Malleus Maleficarum:

a Novel

By James Mather

Dedication

To my sister Sally, without whose help this book never would have been published.

All of the characters in this book are figments of the author's imagination and bear no relation to anyone living or dead.

TABLE OF CONTENTS

PROLOGUE

The gypsy stood facing the tribunal. Her long black hair hung straight down her naked back. The candlelight flickered yellow across her ivory skin.

"Will you confess?"

"I am not a witch."

"Why do your neighbors fear you?"

"My neighbors fear what they do not understand . . . they don't understand many things."

"Why do you dress in black?"

"If your lordships are so interested in my garments, why did you take them from me?"

"We believe the truth."

"The truth is that my neighbors think me wealthy and you think to gain that wealth by declaring me a witch."

"Silence! You impugn the honesty of the Court and through it, the Church. That is heresy!"

"Heretic or witch, you will have your way."

The hooded figure at the center of the tribunal motioned impatiently with his hand. Behind the gypsy a deformed figure in black leather lurched out of the shadows of the stone chamber.

"Show us the marks."

The jailor swung the naked figure around, yanking her raven hair away from her shoulders. Three red marks formed a triangle just below her neck. The leader of the tribunal dismissed the jailor with a gesture. He reluctantly let go of the tender flesh and shuffled back into the shadow.

"Do you deny you are in league with the Devil?"

"I do."

"Where did you get the Devil's mark?"

"I was born with the sign."

"Then you do not deny it?"

"I cannot deny the marks, but I have made no pact with the Devil."

"Do you believe in witchcraft?"

"I believe in your belief in witchcraft else why would I be tried?"

"The Devil's answer!"

"You think to trap me. If I say I believe in witchcraft I am a witch. If I say I do not believe I am a heretic. You can hang me as easily for one as the other."

The hooded figures muttered to one another. The leader could not outsmart the prisoner. Apparently, she knew the book and would not *be tricked into self-incrimination. The leader cursed the ban on torture. They had no such scruples on the continent. An evil smile crept across the hawk-like features of the inquisitor.*

"We must leave your guilt in the hands of God."

The gypsy shuddered. Trials by God invariably meant death or death.

"You will be driven from this place into the wilderness. If you are in league with the Devil, he will succor you. If you are innocent, God will take you to his bosom."

So it was death on the frozen marshes or on the scaffold. The gypsy hung her head as the black robed priests filed out. She glanced up at the empty dais.

The two books lay side by side. <u>The Book of God</u> lay closed. The <u>Malleus Maleficarum</u> was open.

CHAPTER ONE -- CRAB

I

Mary flapped her arms wildly, running down the causeway between the Psychiatric Treatment Center and the Geriatrics Ward. Her cawing sounds echoed from the recesses of the nineteenth century buildings. Paul looked up from his weeding to yell encouragement. "You'll never get off the ground unless you take off into the wind."

Mary wheeled dutifully around and flapped off the other way.

Dr. John smiled at the familiar tableau. He reached for his keys to the octagonal snake pit. The massive key ring held many keys, but he had no trouble picking out the jailor's skeleton key which opened the ancient front door. The stale smell of urine permeated the alcove, but he hardly noticed.

At the nursing station, the young charge nurse was bending over the "red book" checking the third shift report.

"Good morning, Judy . . . anything?"

"Minerva died around three."

John's heart sank and Judy caught the hurt.

"It's for the best."

"I know," said John.

The terminal stages of Huntington's Chorea are not something one prolongs with heroic medical techniques. To say the family was not interested was not wholly accurate. For many long term residents of state hospitals, families lose interest over the years or die off. In the case of Huntington's patients, however, the onset of the disease is accompanied by horror in the rest of the family because of the genetic base of the disease. Since many of the younger members of the family are still at risk, denial sets in and the family will not visit their afflicted relative. The deterioration is horrible to witness and usually fairly rapid. Unlike classic senility, Huntington's disease leaves cognitive function intact for much of the course of the disease so the patient must watch the progression of his own deterioration. In the early stages, suicide is quite common. All in all, John was in agreement with Judy's analysis that Minerva was better off. Yet, even after years of working the Geriatrics ward, where death was inevitable and relatively frequent, John never got over the hurt he felt with every loss.

John glanced longingly at his office, but resisted the urge to retreat into his "cave" as the nurses called it and began making rounds. He had made a habit of coming in early while the third shift was going off duty. The "changing of the guard" occupied the staff and the patients were free to talk before the breakfast routine began. His ten-hour day had escaped the notice of the unions and management for different reasons. The union members, never coming a minute early or leaving a minute late, assumed he worked the same hours as the first shift nursing, unpaid overtime being outside the mainstream of their usual consideration. Management, on the other hand, keeping banking hours, were not around to witness John's arrival at 6:30AM. All of this suited John down to the ground because he was an early morning person anyway and the house held few attractions since Gypsy had left. Of all the sadness surrounding her departure from his life, the saddest was that he didn't even enjoy spending time in his own house anymore.

The Geriatrics Ward was a giant figure eight. The two female wards were on the south portion of the figure and the two male wards were on the north. The main nursing station and clinical offices were in the center. The building was the second oldest structure on the hospital grounds, dating back to the late eighteen hundreds. Built like a fortress, the brick walls were two feet thick with iron bars at the windows and tunnels connecting it to the Administration Building and all of the other structures on the grounds. The State had been threatening to tear it down for years, but it was so solidly constructed the costs of demolition were prohibitive.

John began his rounds on Female One, where the higher functioning, ambulatory residents sat in rows on wooden benches waiting for breakfast. A tiny wizened old lady sat by the door to the Cafeteria. "Good morning, Ruth. How are you?" said John cordially.

"God damn son-of-a-bitch," hissed Ruth.

"Yes, probably. But how are you?"

"What the hell do you care?"

"I care," sighed John and moved on.

Sally had her group arranged in a circle. She always reminded John of a volunteer, with her Mennonite cap and starched gingham dress. As the years had gone by, Sally's world became more and more restricted. Now it was all a Sunday School class. She would usually cajole or coerce five or six of the ladies into taking part. John was struck by the paradox of Mrs. Leiberman, a regular, singing "Jesus loves me" with such gusto.

"Good morning, ladies."

"Good morning, Reverend. Have you come to begin service?"

"No, Sally, this is Monday."

"Nonsense, it's Sunday. I always have Sunday School at nine o'clock. Look . . . all the girls are here."

John didn't argue. Sally was the oldest woman in the hospital. She would be 100 in a month. If she believed she was in Sunday School, what harm? The only time a problem arose was when she was too aggressive in "Bringing in the Sheaves". The other ladies were not always willing participants.

One of the recent trends in therapy was "reality orientation." Growing out of the rehabilitation model of the Veterans Administration hospitals, the idea was to reinforce orientation to person, place, and time. When the cognitive functions begin to fail in the elderly, the patient loses orientation in these three cognitive spheres. with place and time going first and finally personal identity. The process can be slowed and even reversed in some cases by constant reminders of the day, the time, the place and other aspects of the day-to-day activities and environment. "Reality orientation boards" were strategically placed throughout the unit. "This is the Lancaster State Hospital. Today is Monday the 23rd of April. The weather is fair. The next meal is breakfast." Sally's Sunday School group did not conform to, nor reinforce these orienting facts. John was torn between reality orientation and patient interaction. On balance, Sally's group, while not reality oriented, seemed better than the low level of patient interaction typical on the ward. John continued on before Sally pressed him for a sermon.

He slowed down as he reached the end of the long semicircular ward. He kept his eye warily on Bertha as she sat, seemingly asleep in the corner. Suddenly she exploded out of her chair, hurling herself toward the now fully braced Psychologist.

"Murderer! Murderer! I *know* you!" she screamed.

John grabbed her outstretched arms and, as gently as he could, held her until the rage receded and the stuperous look returned to her broad face. "Calm down, Bertha. It's all right."

Bertha went docilely back to her chair and resumed her Buddha-like trance.

John slipped quickly out of the door before the cycle could start again. The first few times Bertha had knocked him down, but he was on to her now. Or was it the reverse? Whose behavior was being modified? Sometimes John wondered if he was becoming as institutionalized as the residents. It was hard to know what normal behavior was anymore. When he first started working at the hospital, the bizarre behavior startled and sometimes shocked him. Now he accepted . . . expected it.

The dark cubicle between the wards was damp, stalagmites, or was it stalactites, he could never remember which were which, oozing from the ancient cement in the ceiling. The circular metal grid stairway ascended into a lighter gloom above and a darker gloom below. John shuddered. Poe's classic "The Cask of Amontillado" raised dark images in John's mind.

As a child, John read voraciously and omnivorously. Poe was one of his favorites and was at least partly responsible for his becoming a psychologist. He was fascinated with the macabre and the murky depths of the minds of Poe's characters. In college, he found in Freud's theory of the unconscious explanations of the abnormal personalities in Poe's works. He had evolved beyond a Freudian interpretation of Personality in Graduate School and found little use for psychoanalysis in his work with psychotics and the elderly, but his analysis of personality still held to many of Freud's principles and his fascination with the macabre remained. The war within him between the metaphysical and the scientific had its most serious consequence in his stormy relationship with Illanna. To her, there was no boundary between science and metaphysics. His rigid adherence to science had forced her to leave and he found little solace in logic to make up for her loss.

John leaned back against the damp wall, gathering his resources for the next ward. He opened the door and walked into a scene which could have been taken from Dante's Inferno. Gerichairs lined both walls. Coarse guttural cries resounded like echoes back and forth between the residents. Huntington's and various other organic patients tore at their clothes, slapped the chairs and themselves or rocked aimlessly in confinement.

"Dear God." The thought, more a prayer than a blasphemy, came for the thousandth time to John's lips and stopped short of expression.

He pitied the ones most who still showed signs of recognition as he passed, greeting each one. His trained clinician's face did not betray the feeling. John had on his ministerial smile and held it as if his face would crack if he changed expression. With the "organics" behind him, John brightened and continued through the ladies' non-ambulatory ward.

"Here comes the head-shrinker!" cackled Betty.

John laughed.

"Your head looks the same size as last week, Betty."

Betty flashed a toothless grin from her half-raised bed.

"You can't get inside my head, Dr. John."

"I'd like to, Betty. I bet I'd find some pretty interesting things in there."

John walked beside the bed and gave her a hug.

"How's the ward?"

"Pretty quiet, except for the new one. She cried all night."

"I better go and have a talk with her," said John, kissing Betty affectionately on the cheek.

Curled in the fetal position and racked with sobs, the tiny form was lost in the large crib-like bed.

John remembered the name from the intake forms.

"Hello, Mrs. Gutshalt."

The form straightened and rolled toward him. Two red-rimmed eyes peered at him from the hollow face.

"Who are you?"

"Dr. John Lowell. I'm the psychologist here. How can I help you?"

"I want to go home."

"I know you do," said John kindly.

Mrs. Gutshalt didn't have a home. The husband she cried for had been dead for twenty years. She had been sleeping in the park and eating garbage for weeks before the police found her half dead in the gutter. John's mind checked back over the admission papers.

"Betty tells me you've been crying."

"They won't let my husband come to see me."

"It's not visiting hours," said John evasively. "Have you been eating?"

The chart showed a weight gain of three pounds. The emaciated form didn't seem to have three pounds of flesh on it.

"I'm not hungry."

"You have to eat so you can get strong and have visitors." John felt like a rat when he said this, because he knew that any visitors Mrs. Gutshalt would get would have to be manufactured from the legion of volunteers. But you can't work with a corpse. If visitors would keep her eating, then John would use the leverage. Get them back into the land of the living, then work on the problems.

"I'll be coming by from time to time. I hope we'll get to know each other better."

Mrs. Gutshalt didn't smile, but she wasn't crying either. "Small gains, small gains," John repeated to himself as a litany.

II

Judy North was dispensing medications when John finished his rounds on the women's side. The medicine cart was lined with paper cups holding a myriad of pills and liquids for the morning routine. John stopped to talk to her about the new patient.

"How's Mrs. Gutshalt doing?"

"She's eating better, but she's still dehydrated."

"Has she had a physical?"

"Not yet."

John grunted in irritation. "She's supposed to have a physical within 24 hours of admission."

Judy shrugged. "Dr. Azahdi hasn't been in yet. He was gone by the time she came in Friday."

"When is he due in this morning?"

"He's the O.D. He should have been in with us on the first shift," she said, glancing at her watch.

"Who's covering?"

"There might be a doctor on one of the other units."

"Might be? That's a hell of a way to run a hospital."

"Don't get mad at me, John. I was here on time."

"I know, I'm sorry. I shouldn't take it out on you. But it's dangerous not having doctors around with these patients."

"We've been through all that, John. Who's going to lean on them? They have a sweetheart deal with the clinical director so they can do their private practice on State time. They can work anywhere, and without them on the roster, we lose accreditation and Medicare."

"What good is accreditation if the patients aren't being treated?"

"It's a paper game, John. You should be used to it by now."

"I'll never get used to it."

John crossed over to the men's side of the figure eight. The men were generally lower functioning than the women, but John felt more comfortable on these wards.

The ambulatory ward was half empty. There were fewer men to begin with, and many of the ones on this ward were already out with the grounds crew working. Bill and Sam were playing checkers in the day room.

"Bill . . . Sam, how's it going?"

"Sam cheats," said Bill, turning.

"I do not," said Sam, moving several pieces behind Bill's back.

"You scoundrel," chided John.

Sam smiled, tobacco running down his stubbled chin.

"He beats me all the time anyway."

"I've got the winner," John quipped over his shoulder as he moved on.

At the far end of the ward, a sudden commotion sent John running. Ted, a black aide, was banging desperately at one of the bedroom doors.

"Who's in there?" John yelled.

"I think it's Abe!"

Ted pushed against the metal door with his shoulder.

"He's got something wedged against the door!"

"He's suicidal!" yelled John, looking for something to pry open the door.

For once he cursed housekeeping for keeping the ward too neat. There was nothing lying around. The seconds were ticking away, and John knew the clock was against them. The terrazzo floor was too slippery to get a good foothold. John ran into the next bedroom and dragged a bed back with him. Wedging it lengthwise against the opposite wall, it came within three feet of the blocked door. The two men braced against the bed and pushed at the door. It began to move slowly and then more rapidly as they gained momentum. With a foot of clearance, John squeezed into the room past the bed and locker that had been obstructing the door. Abe hung kicking above the bed, his belt around the automatic sprinkler pipe and his neck.

"Jesus!" John pushed up on Abe's legs.

"Get that belt off him!"

Ted pulled himself up on the locker and loosened the loop around Abe's neck, pulling it over his head. Abe slumped down knocking John to the bed. John pulled him onto the floor, cleared his mouth with his fingers and started mouth-to-mouth resuscitation. Ted was shifting from one leg to the other, wringing his hands. John looked up in exasperation.

"Get Judy!" he gasped between breaths. "And oxygen!"

He bent back over Abe, hearing Ted's running footsteps receding toward the nursing station. It was less than a minute, but it seemed like an eternity until John heard the clank of the oxygen cart returning. Judy and Ted pushed the bed out of the way and brought in the oxygen equipment. In a few minutes, the horrible blue receded from Abe's face, and he was breathing normally.

"Any doctor go to male one . . . any doctor go to male one . . . emergency." The intercom added its anti-climax. Judy looked up. "I wonder who will come to save his life?"

Now that it was all over, John began to shake. He had to get back to his office.

"Will you and Ted make out the special incident report?"

Judy nodded.

"Thanks." John shouldered his way through the crowd of patients and staff. Sitting behind his desk, he fought down a wave of nausea.

John's office was more like a professor's than a clinician's. Books lined the walls from ceiling to floor and were strewn open on the tables and chairs. John himself had the rumpled absent-minded professorial look. The nurses had nicknamed him "Sugar Bear." He was a bear of a man, five-foot-ten and two hundred and twenty five pounds. The sugar came from his disposition which, with a few notable exceptions, was generally sweet. The nurses had nicknames for almost everyone in the hospital, but he was one of the few who knew what his was.

Gradually calm returned as John sat in an instinctive trancelike state. He waited for the inevitable buzzer. At 10:00 it came. John depressed the local button and picked up the phone.

"I want you in my office right now!" The scream came over the phone.

"I'm busy." John slammed down the receiver. He could play out the scene in his head. The Crab would be running out of his office to yell at his secretary. She would go to the nursing station. Judy should be coming over about now.

The timid knock was right on schedule.

"Please talk to him, John, he's in an absolute rage."

"Okay."

John knew that if he didn't the nurses would catch hell all day, and he would just be forestalling an inevitable confrontation anyway. He walked slowly to the Director's office, trying to suppress his anger.

The Crab sat behind his enormous mahogany desk. It dwarfed him, almost coming up to his chin. The Pakistani doctor had been christened the Crab because of his disposition and the way he sidled around never seeming to come straight at anything. He was one of the most devious men John had ever met, incapable of dealing honestly with anything or anybody.

"What going on here? How come hospital ambulance, police cars mob at door!"

"Abe tried to commit suicide."

"I know, but whole world not have to be in on it."

"Some of us were concerned for his life."

"Don't take attitude with me! I medical responsibility around here!"

"Then you better start taking it. We had no medical coverage around here from 6:30AM to 9:30AM."

"Don't tell me job. If Abe suicidal, why he not watched?"

"*If* Abe is suicidal. It's all over his chart. Ted is new, and we are running under minimal coverage on Male One every day. He was in there by himself and had to get everybody off to work. You can't pin this one on him."

"Can't help nurses don't come in."

"They don't come in because the morale is at rock bottom. They don't think anyone gives a damn."

A sly look came over Azahdi's swarthy face.

"Who writing up report?"

"The people on the scene . . . Judy and Ted."

"You there . . . yes?"

"Yes."

"Why you not write report?"

"Why should I?"

"You go easy on suicide business."

John exploded. "Bullshit! Protect your own ass. You were the O.D. and you weren't here. Those doors should have been changed so that they opened out after the Joint Commission's recommendation. Your butt's in the wringer and I'm not saving it."

Azahdi shook with rage. "I have you fired."

"Then God damn it, you better do it fast, and meanwhile stay out of my way or I'll crush you like a bug!"

He slammed the door behind him and stood trembling in the outer office. The receptionist sat rigidly with her back to the door where John stood trying to collect himself. The tension in the room slowly dissolved and Debbie turned toward him.

"'God' called. He wants to see you sometime this morning."

"Debbie, you shouldn't call him 'God'," John scolded. "One of these days, you guys are going to slip and use these nicknames to someone's face."

"That will never happen, Sugar Bear," Debbie purred.

John broke up, laughter washing the tension away. He was still laughing as he passed the nursing station. Judy regarded him curiously. "You're sure in a better mood than you were a couple of minutes ago. I thought you were killing him in there."

"Just a minor disagreement." John smiled, ducking back into his office. Behind his desk, a frown returned as he tried to puzzle pieces together. The Crab worked fast. He must have called Johnson before he called me, but he didn't know we were going to have a fight. He might have been able to get me to falsify the records and get him off the hook. It didn't hang together. John gave up. He decided to take it as it came and just react. He decided to walk the quarter mile to the Administration Building.

Lancaster State Hospital is situated on the edge of the old city. It was begun on the tide of Dorothea Dix's march through Pennsylvania in the middle 1800's. The city proper had not grown much since then, but suburbs had sprung up around the hospital compressing it from its original two thousand acres of farms and woodlands to a mere two hundred acres. From a single building constructed in 1855, it had burgeoned into a complex of over sixty resident wards and ancillary structures. The architecture hadn't change much. Massive brick walls with iron bars at the windows were the rule until the latest buildings constructed in the 1950's. After that, with patient populations plummeting, there was no new construction. Empty monoliths gazed blankly across the central causeway between the Geriatrics Ward and the Administration Building.

Spring was in the air. The cherry blossoms were starting to push on the trees lining the causeway. It was John's favorite time of year at the hospital. The poignancy of so much human misery in the midst of such natural beauty could make you cry. In the spring, residents and staff came out of the locked wards and into the sunlight. Some residents would stay in the sunlight and go home. A few would make it in the community and not return. The air was full of hope and cherry blossoms.

Halfway down the long walk John turned into the patient's store. The regular crew was in having coffee. Henry was sitting at the end of the table.

"Henry, you old reprobate, why aren't you working?" John called across the room.

"Chon! Come have a sip of coffee onct!"

John bought a cup at the counter and sat down next to him. Henry was 83. He was out with the grounds crew every morning at seven o'clock. He had been a farm laborer for 65 years. On his eightieth birthday, he went into Ephrata and got drunk and proceeded to take the town apart. It took most of the local police and a few State cops to get him under control and bring him up to the hospital. Henry adjusted to the hospital as his retirement home. He worked every day till he felt like taking a break at the store. He was regularly decertified as being inappropriate for a psychiatric hospital, but even a hint of placement brought a rage reaction which justified his stay.

"Where are you going, Chon?"

"Administration."

"Me, too. Peggy and me are getting married."

Peggy was the delectable 20-year-old receptionist in the Administration Building.

"What about Anna?"

"She's too old."

Anna was Henry's 40-year old girlfriend in the Long Term Care Center. Henry generally had at least three girls strategically placed around the hospital. Currently, things were a little slow. John looked down the long table. Every moocher in the hospital was there. The ones without jobs panhandled all morning till they had enough money for a doughnut and a cup of coffee. It wasn't quite the mad hatter's tea party, but John wouldn't have been too surprised to see a rabbit at the head of the table. Lord knows what they were seeing.

Mary was talking in a low undertone to the empty chair on her right. George was talking to Mary about a problem he was having with the FBI, the CIA, and his brother, the President. Frank was doing mathematical problems in the air, but must have been making a lot of mistakes because he kept erasing the answers. John shook his head because these were the patients with ground privileges.

"I have to be going, Henry. See you later."

"Tell Peggy I'll be over."

"I will."

John pulled out a cigar and lit up. The Superintendent hated cigars.

If I'm going to be fired, no sense in being pleasant, John thought.

Like a Freudian dream, John would feel his legs moving, but the Administration Building didn't seem to get any closer. Myriads of possibilities swam through his mind as he prepared himself for the coming interview.

Then he was there, and Peggy was smiling brightly.

John spoke first. "Henry's coming over."

Peggy giggled.

It can't be, John thought. But with Henry, who knows? John laid a cigar on the desk. "Give Henry a cigar . . . he won't accept anything from me."

"Sure. You can go right in. Dr. Johnson's expecting you."

CHAPTER TWO — GOD

I

Whenever John entered the Superintendent's office, he felt as though he had stepped through the door of a time machine. The fourteen-foot ceiling was not designed in a century which was concerned with energy conservation. The hand-carved wood paneling was not made by union labor. The long, polished mahogany conference table leading up to the dais looked like a Hollywood set for a Richard the Lion-Hearted movie. "God" sat behind his enormous desk on his . . . well, it wasn't really a throne . . . it just looked like one. His long, flowing hair and beard didn't belong to this Century either, or the last, but to eternity.

"Come in, John. We have a problem."

"Yes?" John wasn't going to be helpful.

"This was on my desk when I came in this morning."

Now John *was* curious. The jungle telegram was fast, but the mail was notoriously slow. The note couldn't be related to the morning's events. Dr. Johnson pushed the crumpled paper across the desk. John smoothed it out and began to read.

Subject: Presence of Foreign Devils on our Soil

To: Hospital Superintendent Dr. Gardner Johnson

From: Malleus Maleficarum

I will not tolerate foreign interference with my people's well-being. My master, the prince of darkness, has decreed all foreigners shall be expelled, or there will be a blood bath cleansing this sacred earth.

"What do you think of it? A joke?"

"If it is, it's not a very good one," John answered.

"Who do you think wrote it?"

John's analytic mind began checking off the possibilities. "Assuming it's a joke, it's almost certainly from an employee. It's on hospital memo paper and typed. It's a fairly easy operation for an employee to produce it and not as easy but possible for him to plant it. On the other hand, it's unlikely that it is a joke. One: it's a serious matter if he's caught . . . probably would lose him his job. Two: it's too enigmatic to be funny, unless it relates to an inside joke which you know about . . . does it?"

"No."

"Then let's assume it's meant seriously. From an operational point of view, it's a better assumption anyway. If it's genuine, it has the ominous trappings of a paranoid threat. The writer is either a patient or a staff member who should be a patient. The qualifications of access to the paper, typewriter, and your office still apply, but patients cannot be ruled out. A talented paranoid could pull it off almost as easily as a staff member. In fact, being here 24 hours a day (legitimately) security would not question his presence on hospital grounds on any shift, providing he had a reasonable excuse for being where he was. An administrative type here after 4:00PM or before 8:00AM would stick out like a sore thumb."

Johnson combed his hand through his white beard. "Do you think it's a paranoid schizophrenic?"

John was non-committal. "That's hard to tell. It would be easier if it were handwritten. The handwriting might tell us the degree of decompensation. It's a little too short, coherent and to the point for a paranoid schizophrenic, but that might be a product of the amount of time he had at the typewriter."

"He?"

"Well, it could be a woman of course," John admitted. "But it certainly sounds masculine on the face of it."

"What do you think we ought to do about it?"

John was flattered by the Superintendent's reliance on his judgment. He was not really surprised. Many times in the past, in difficult clinical situations, Johnson had come to him for advice. His trust had developed over the last few years in watching John's performance at Court hearings. John had evidenced a rare combination of clinical acumen and practicality in dealing with very complex situations. "We can't expel the foreign devils or even protect them. It is not clear from the memo what the 'home' nationality is, much less the definition of a foreigner. Assuming the *nation* is the hospital, we still don't know if foreigner is meant literally (we certainly have enough non-U.S. citizens around) or meant in terms of community people or even staff. It seems that all we *can* do is to try and figure out who Malleus Maleficarum is."

Johnson nodded. "How would you go about it?"

"Staff members are tough, but we have considerable information on patients and their delusions. Malleus may just turn up in the records."

"Would you try and find out?"

John paused. His regular duties didn't leave much time for ---what the hell---witch hunts. Dr. Johnson saw the reluctance.

"I know it's a lot of trouble John, but I have a bad feeling about this. I will give you released time from your other duties and clear it with Dr. Azahdi."

John grimaced at the mention of his Director.

"I know about the scrape this morning. I'll take care of that, too."

"Okay."

II

Quite a morning. Was it only noon? John thought back over the day's events as he headed for the gym. Minerva, Abe, the Crab and now Malleus. Whenever things began to pile up, John sought exercise. The simple physical confrontation of pain and exertion put mental confusion into perspective. The gym stood adjacent to the Geriatrics Ward, with the Extended Care Center to the north. Architecturally, it was considered more modern than the other buildings on campus, having been constructed only twenty-five years earlier. *Mens sana in corpore sano.* Malleus had John thinking in Latin.

The weight room was a twenty-by-twenty foot annex to the main gymnasium. Some of the staff were playing half-court basketball and called out to John as he headed for his locker.

"Come on, John, play a little basketball."

John chuckled. He was notoriously the worst basketball player at the hospital. He played in the local tournaments and was known as "the hammer" because his style in basketball was identical to his style in football. In neither sport did he ever try to go around anyone. It usually took about three minutes of play for him to foul out. By that time, however, the other team was generally out of substitutes.

John got into his old sweats and began to warm up. The Universal Gym occupied the center of the room. Various instruments of torture were scattered around the walls. With the pin set at two hundred pounds, he began to stretch out his pectoral muscles with sets of ten repetitions on the bench. He looked up as Randy sidled through the door.

Conventional doors were not designed for Randy. John often thought that the concept of misfit had been invented for him. His clothes didn't fit. He didn't fit the furniture and had to go sideways through doors. Randy was five feet three inches tall and weighed two hundred and seventy-five pounds. His shortened arms and bowed legs made him look like a giant dwarf, a concept of Tolkien's that John had some problems with. He rolled like a sailor when he walked and always had a wide grin on his face. "Hi Doc."

"Hi, Randy. How's she hanging?"

Randy jumped in on alternate sets. With his massive chest and short arms, he only had to push the weight around four inches to lock out. After a couple of sets, he had the pin up to the maximum weight of the Universal and still hadn't worked up a sweat. He moved over to the standard bench and loaded up the Olympic bar to 450 pounds. John spotted him as he easily knocked out five repetitions.

Randy was diagnosed manic depressive, manic type. He had been stabilized on Lithium Carbonate before John got him into weight lifting. John had talked the psychiatrist into taking Randy off the medication and channeling his manic energy into exercise. The staff was vehemently against Randy lifting weights when John first suggested it. They were afraid of him and argued that they didn't need him being any stronger than he was. John reminded them that he was already more than anyone could handle and added strength would not change that situation. They howled again when he was taken off the medication, but so far the program was working out well.

In addition to his psychosis, Randy had severe problems in relating to people because of his body image. He felt that he was a freak and that people were constantly laughing at him. John was making progress in this area also. Randy could relate to John because he was also atypical. In contrast to Randy, however, John projected the feeling that he was more or less proud of his outrageous dimensions. Using John as a role model, Randy was beginning to develop pride in his own strength and lose some of his shyness.

The workout had John going from station to station on the Universal, with Randy trailing along after. In 45 minutes, all the upper body muscles were exhausted. John rolled over on the mat feeling the "pump" gradually receding. Randy ambled toward the door.

"I'm going to lunch."

"See you later."

John started mentally gearing up for his run. He had also tried to convince the staff that a jogging club should be developed for the patients. Here he had met a resistance which he had been unable to break through. The image of running patients meant only one thing to staff who were still trying to adjust to the new laws requiring less restrictive conditions for residents. Running and runaways were synonymous and no amount of logical argument could persuade them.

John started off slowly, gaining momentum as he headed for the front gate. It was a miracle that no accidents had ever resulted from his daily emergence from the grounds. The hulking figure with monk-like hooded sweatshirt and grisly beard invariably caused rubber-necking double takes among the motorists. The State Hospital sign over the gate and the charging apparition formed a surrealistic image.

John had been running since it wasn't popular and paid very little attention to the impression he was making. He continued along the main road past the other State buildings. The land

which climbed the long hill beside the
hospital grounds veered off to the right. John
began chugging up the gradual incline. In the
middle of the hill, the grade was steep. His
breath came faster and faster. Every third
step, every second step, every step. Now he
was at the crest and started the slow decline
around the back of the hospital grounds. A
spring chill was in the air even at the noon
hour, but John was soaked with sweat. The
pain in his lungs subsided and he began to
feel his legs cramping up as he fought the
downhill grade. As he turned the corner of the
Geriatrics Building, he came up short.
Another ambulance and several police cars
were at the front entrance. Now what? Abe
was in the General Hospital by now.

This was not routine with all the police cars.
He coasted to a stop and went into the nursing
station. Judy sat white-faced behind her
desk.

"What is it?", asked John.

"Dr. Azahdi is dead."

"What! How did it happen?"

"We don't know. Debbie found him. His neck
is broken."

"An accident?"

"It doesn't look like it. A detective is coming
from downtown."

"I'm going over to the gym and change. I'll be back in fifteen minutes."

John's mind was racing. Had someone actually killed the Crab? Was it Malleus? When did it happen? How did it happen with so many people around? No answers emerged. The hot shower relaxed his muscles and quieted his mental state. By the time he got back to the ward, he was ready to approach the situation rationally. A young man in a gray suit was leaning over the half-door of the nursing station talking to Judy. "Here's Dr. Lowell now. Dr. Lowell, this is Detective Schneider."

"How do you do, Doctor. May I talk to you for a few minutes?"

"Sure. Come on into my office."

The detective followed John into the room. John cleared some books off the chair facing the desk and Schneider sat down. John waited. Schneider studied him a moment.

"What do you know about this matter?"

"What matter?" John decided to be obtuse.

"Dr. Azahdi's death."

"Only what Judy told me. That he was dead with a broken neck."

"Did you know that you were the last person to see him alive?"

"I didn't and don't know that and neither do you."

"What do you mean?"

"It depends entirely on how he died. If he was murdered, and you must suspect that or we wouldn't be having this conversation, then the *murderer* was the last person to see him alive."

"I see your point."

"And I see yours."

The two men appraised each other. Both were trained observers, good at their jobs. They observed different things, however. Schneider saw a man powerfully built, unusually calm under the circumstances who was unlikely to be trapped or give anything away he didn't want to. John saw an intelligent suspicious man, but, beneath the surface, he sensed an uneasiness which was unnatural. The smell of fear was on Schneider, not the fear of patients which was common to community people unused to the State Hospital, but something deeper.

"The receptionist said that you and Azahdi had a violent argument this morning. She did not see or hear him after that argument until she went in with his mail at 1:00. He was dead, slumped over his desk with a broken neck."

"I question the use of the term violent. It was a bad argument but no violence was involved."

"What were you arguing about?"

"I'm not sure it concerns you. It certainly does not relate to his death."

"I would like to be the judge of that."

John considered the ethics involved. It was not a violation of Abe's rights or breach of confidentiality as the suicide attempt was already a matter of record with the police. Criticism of Azahdi was certainly of no concern to Azahdi any longer.

"We had an attempted suicide this morning."

"I know about that."

"Dr. Azahdi and I disagreed about whose fault it was and what should be done about it."

"Would you elaborate on that?"

"Azahdi said that Abe wasn't being watched closely enough and that we should soft pedal the attempt in the medical records."

"And what was your response?"

"I pointed out that he was supposed to be the medical man on duty and that he had not been here. I also reminded him that the recommendation for changing the doors so that they opened out instead of in was made over a year ago."

"I understand that you also threatened him."

"Did Debbie say that?"

Schneider hesitated. "Not exactly. She said that she couldn't understand all the words through the door."

"Well, I did."

"You did?"

"If I remember correctly, I said that if he didn't stay out of my way I'd crush him like a bug."

"Are you in the habit of threatening people with physical violence?"

"It's just an expression."

"An expression which coincidentally seems to be a fairly accurate description of what happened to Dr. Azahdi."

"I didn't kill him."

"I'm glad to hear it but you must admit things do not look too good at this point."

"I admit to nothing of the kind. You are welcome to your view, but I have a somewhat different perspective."

"What is that?"

"I *know* I didn't do it."

"You will be available for further questions?"

"If that is a preamble to the usual speech ·
about leaving town, the answer is no, I am not
leaving town, and yes, I will be around for
further questions during my regular hours."

"Thank you."

Schneider left John sitting behind his desk
staring at the door. So *he* was the chief
suspect! An interesting turn of events and one
which certainly added an imperative to the
quest for Malleus, if Malleus was in fact
involved. But who else could it be?

III

Schneider sat in his car in front of the Administration Building, trying to pull himself together. Sweat poured off his narrow face, seeping into his collar. His hands jerked uncontrollably whenever he let go of the steering wheel. He pressed his forehead against the cold, knurled plastic.

"Oh God, Mother," he sobbed.

No one would ever know the superhuman effort required for him to appear calm during his interview with John Lowell. He knew now that he could maintain at least that outward composure . . . if he didn't see *her*. He certainly couldn't meet with the Superintendent in this condition. Gradually, he felt himself relaxing. In a few minutes he would be ready.

Peggy appraised the pale handsome detective. There was a poet's suffering in those dark eyes which brought out the maternal instinct in most women. Peggy was no exception, but she maintained a cool professional manner.

"You may go right in."

Dr. Johnson got up from behind his desk and ushered Schneider to an alcove overlooking the front lawn.

"Very distressing. I was afraid something like this might happen."

Johnson didn't look distressed. An aura of calm always surrounded him. Schneider felt himself drawn into it and began to relax.

"You were expecting a murder?"

"Not exactly."

"What then?"

"I found this note on my desk this morning."

He pushed the note across the table to Schneider. The detective held it gingerly by the edges.

"Don't worry, it's already been . . . what do you call it? . . . dusted for prints by our Security."

Schneider grimaced. He didn't have much respect for the expertise of security police.

"I would like to have my lab boys go over it in any event if that's acceptable."

"Certainly."

Schneider read the note through several times. "It doesn't make much sense to me."

"It didn't make much sense to us either, but, unfortunately, it's beginning to."

"Us?"

"I showed the note to Dr. Lowell."

"That's funny. I just talked to Dr. Lowell and he didn't mention it."

"Maybe he didn't see any connection."

"Dr. Lowell did not impress me as a stupid man."

Johnson laughed. "No, stupid he's not. But you must understand we are all very careful about patient behavior and communicating our suppositions to anyone not involved in patient treatment."

"Then you have concluded that the note is from a patient?"

"I think it is. John doesn't seem too sure. In any event I have asked him to see if he can find Malleus."

"I'm afraid that is now a job for us professionals."

Dr. Johnson studied Schneider for a moment before he replied. "You are probably good at your job and are certainly professional. We are also good at our jobs and are also professionals. You will be searching for the man; we will be searching for his mind."

"I hope our purposes will not be in conflict."

"They shouldn't be. I will tell John to cooperate with you in whatever way he can."

"Thank you." Schneider headed back to Geriatrics.

IV

A soft knock came at John's door.

"Come in."

Debbie squeezed into the room and stood against the wall. She was pale and shaking.

"What is it, Debbie?"

"John, I *lied* to him."

"Who?"

"Schneider."

"You mean about the argument?"

"No – yes, that too, but about my being at my desk."

"How do you mean?"

"I told him that I was out on break part of the time after you left."

"Well?"

"John, I wasn't! I didn't leave my desk until Frank brought in the mail and then I took it right into, into . . ." Debbie began to cry.

John got up and put his arm around her.

"Don't cry. It's all right."

Debbie sobbed. "You didn't kill him, did you, John?"

"No."

Debbie's tears subsided.

"I can't get into any trouble, can I?"

"You weren't under oath. You can change your statement later if he presses you."

"But John, how could anyone get in there? There is only the one door."

"I don't know. But someone must have, unless the Crab broke his own neck."

Debbie looked at him reproachfully. "You shouldn't speak of him like that now he's dead."

"You're right. I didn't like him, but I'm sorry he's dead."

Debbie turned to go. John said, "Thank you, Debbie. But don't lie anymore. We'll figure out what happened. It will be all right." The door closed softly behind her.

Now John was really puzzled. When Schneider picks up on that! How could anyone get in there? He had to take a closer look at that office.

John opened the door a crack. There were no policemen in the central hall. He walked over to the nursing station.

"Are they gone?", asked John.

"They just left. I think Schneider's going over to see 'God'," said Judy.

"I'm going to take a look in Azahdi's office."

"Schneider told me not to let anyone in there."

"Come on, Judy."

"Okay." Judy handed him the master key from her desk. John went through the outer office. Debbie looked up startled, but John put his finger to his lips and went around her in the inner door. She didn't protest and he entered Azahdi's office. He half expected to see the Crab slumped across his desk, but he was gone of course. The room was the same as when he had been in earlier, as far as he could determine. The furniture was undisturbed, papers scattered on the desk but in a more-or-less purposeful way. John looked around the office. The only immediate possibility of entrance was the window. He examined it carefully. It was barred on the outside with a lock toward the office. The lock looked as though it hadn't been opened for many years. The dust on the window sill was undisturbed. Houdini couldn't have come in that way. The only other door in the room was the closet. John opened it and peered around the small room. Nothing. No trap door, nothing in the ceiling.

John heard the latch on the outer door and whirled around.

"Returning to the scene of the crime?" A uniformed officer scowled at him. "Please go back to your office and wait until Detective Schneider returns."

John went sheepishly back to his desk. Now he was in the soup. Schneider would want to know why he went in there. If he told him about the access, Debbie was in trouble and he was in bigger trouble. He'd have to concoct something temporarily. Oh, what a tangled web . . .

V

"I'm disappointed in you, Doctor." Schneider looked peeved. "You're not playing by the rules."

"I didn't know there were rules."

"You are interfering with a police investigation and that's a criminal offense."

"I didn't interfere with anything. I simply went into a colleague's office."

"Against my express orders. Why?"

"You don't give the orders around here . . ." Now John was getting angry. "We have a job to do which goes beyond the purview of your investigation." Just the right touch of righteous indignation, John thought. Schneider was not so easily put off by the smoke screen.

"What did you want in there?"

"Just morbid curiosity. Wanted to see the place where, etc."

"I don't believe you."

"That's your privilege."

The two men stared at each other . . . the moment becoming long and uncomfortable. Schneider broke the icy silence.

"What's all this about Malleus . . . (he looked at his notebook) . . .?"

"Maleficarum? You've discussed the note with the Superintendent?"

"Yes."

"Then you know as much about it as we do."

"Not quite. What does Malleus Maleficarum mean?"

This was better. They were on John's turf, and he went into his professional mode. "The Malleus Maleficarum is a book first published in 1486. It has had many subsequent publications and is probably the most significant work on witchcraft ever written. The two authors, Jakob Sprenger and Heinrich Kramer, were both German inquisitors who received their authority from Pope Innocent the VIIIth. The book is divided into three parts. The first part proselytizes for belief in witchcraft and argues that disbelief is, in fact, heretical. Part two relates the various types of evil, *maleficia*, witches engage in. These involve making a compact with the devil, sexual involvement with devils, casting curses on one's fellowman and so on. Part three gives step by step procedures for trying, obtaining convictions, and sentencing witches."

"I don't understand. What has this to do with insanity?"

John winced, "Mental disability?"

Schneider shrugged.

"The history of mental illness and man's perception of it is a fascinating one. Previous to the middle ages, many of the recognized types of mental illness were thought to befall an unfortunate who was relatively blameless for his condition. Some of the cures were rather gruesome, because one of the concepts behind exorcism is that you make the body such an uninhabitable place that even the devil can't stand it and departs. An example was the custom of lowering a person into a pit full of snakes to literally scare the devil out of him. That is, by the way, where the term 'snake pit,' in reference to mental hospitals, comes from."

Schneider shuddered. "Go on."

"During the same period, there grew a widespread belief in witchcraft spawned, like all superstition, by ignorance, particularly of the causality of natural events. People had to have someone to blame for storms and drought, plagues and famines. They didn't understand what caused these events, so they blamed the witches.

"Gradually, demonic possession got confused with making a pact with the devil. This was an ominous turn of events for the mentally afflicted person. Whereas he had previously been blameless in his transaction with the devil, he now had an active part and was therefore a heretic to be punished rather than a victim to be cured. God knows how many of the several hundred thousand "witches" burned at the stake were actually schizophrenics." John paused.

"This person who calls himself Malleus Maleficarum. How does that fit in?"

"That is very difficult to say because of the way in which the paranoid mind operates. Paranoid systems are generally internally consistent. The logical presentation of the book, Malleus Maleficarum, and its scope would appear to the paranoid in the same way that any major treatise would. The Bible, for example, is the most common base for paranoid systems. What makes interpretation difficult is that the basic premises of the paranoid are usually quite delusional, so we don't know, at least not yet, where Malleus is coming from . . . what the book means to him."

"Do you think this Malleus, whoever he may be, was involved in Dr. Azahdi's death?"

"I don't know. Without identifying him and working with him, I can't tell whether the memo was an action-oriented or non-action-oriented threat."

"But if you found him you could tell?"

"Probably."

Schneider didn't look convinced. John understood the skepticism.

"I couldn't provide evidence which would be satisfactory to the judicial system, but I could be fairly certain of the potential for violence and the probable linkage between delusional and acting out behavior."

"So you are going to look for Malleus?"

"Not for the reason you think."

"And what is that?"

"You're thinking that I'm on the spot and that Malleus is my out. I promised Dr. Johnson I would try to find Malleus before I knew about Azahdi. Whoever wrote the note, patient or staff, needs help and could be dangerous."

"You don't even know if it's a patient?" Schneider was incredulous.

"I have some problems with it being a patient . . . yes."

"Why?"

"You have to have some grasp of the nature of paranoia and its relationship to psychotic and non-psychotic states."

"Which is?"

"Paranoia itself is not a unitary concept. It contains elements of persecutory and/or grandiose delusions. If Malleus suffers from a mental disorder, and, in the broadest sense of mental disorder, he almost certainly does, then he is some form of paranoid. His note contains both of the classic elements of paranoia. The reference to 'his people' and his relationship to the 'Devil' is grandiose, while 'interference' by 'foreigners' is persecutory. The problem is that the note appears to be too well integrated to be authored by a schizophrenic."

"What do you mean?"

"Paranoid schizophrenics, of which we have a relatively large number here at the hospital, generally do not have well-integrated delusional systems. They are not complex and they keep changing. Even those who did would not have the control or insight to hide their delusions under a bushel."

"I don't understand."

"Malleus would *call* himself Malleus and we would know who he is."

"What about other forms of paranoia?"

"Ah . . . there it gets interesting. We can rule out *paranoid state* for some of the same reasons as paranoid schizophrenic. In the paranoid state the delusional system is not well integrated. Also, the elements of grandiosity are not likely to be present."

"Are there other forms?"

"Yes, I have saved the best for last. The true paranoid. Paranoia is a relatively rare psychotic disorder which usually develops over many years. It involves a very elaborate and internally consistent system with both of the elements of persecution and grandiosity. What makes it the prime candidate for Malleus' disorder is that the particular form does not interfere with the rest of the person's personality. Malleus would be able and, in fact, would purposely hide his identity from the world of 'foreigners'."

"But then he would not appear psychotic."

"Exactly."

"But you have ruled out a patient here as being Malleus."

"No."

"What?"

"You underestimate the paranoid. The very nature of the illness requires above average intelligence. You cannot be as logical and consistent as a paranoid and not have superior intellectual gifts. It is not at all unusual for a paranoid to be in the upper one percent of the population on IQ tests."

"What difference does that make?"

"If you were a bright paranoid and you wanted to hide the craziness that only you knew you had, where would be a good place?"

"The hospital!"

"Yes . . . masquerading as a garden variety schizophrenic."

"Why a schizophrenic? Why not some other disorder further from the real one?"

"It's possible that the paranoid could masquerade as any of the psychotics but unlikely. The paranoid is in a quandary similar to that of Benjamin Franklin. Ben said that he could achieve all things but humility, because if he ever achieved it, it would make him proud. The paranoid needs to show his intelligence, and only the role of paranoid schizophrenic would give him the proper arena. Also, masquerading as a lower functioning patient would be very dangerous. There is nothing as difficult for an intelligent person to do as behave stupidly all the time. He would be bound to slip sooner or later. No . . . Malleus could be anyone . . . a patient, a member of the staff, volunteer . . ."

"Or a psychologist," Schneider added.

John smiled. "Or a psychologist."

CHAPTER THREE -- GYPSY

I

John eased his battered XKE around the corner onto the tree-lined street. Post World War II ranchers stood in identical lines behind the close-cropped sycamores. The only distinguishing feature of John's house was the hairy lawn and hedges. He had given up long ago competing in the local clipping and edging contest. The neighbors tolerated the rumpled landscape about as well as the rumpled psychologist. A psychedelic van was parked in front of the unkempt property. John smiled. "Gypsy's back in town."

The welcome mat was pushed slightly to one side, and John knew the door would be unlocked. He opened it quietly and crossed the narrow foyer into the living rom. Gypsy sat in front of the low altar. Her dark hair hanging to her waist contrasted with the flowing white robe and covered most of the multi-colored sash. She rocked in rhythm to the Latin cadence she recited in a monotone. The green candles cast flickering shadows in the darkened room. John waited motionless until she stopped and turned toward him. She was smiling, but tears were still wet on her cheeks. She rose and moved quickly toward him, burying her head in his shoulder.

"Welcome home."

"I had to come back."

"I know. I'm glad."

He lifted her as if she were a child and carried her upstairs.

Illanna slipped onto the floor of John's bedroom and looked hard into his eyes. Her breath came quickly and a familiar flush came to her pale cheeks. "I want you, John."

John's answer caught in his throat as she dropped her white robe to the floor. He pulled her close enveloping her in his powerful arms. She moved, tearing at his clothes and pulling him toward the bed. The months of separation translated into frenzy and then tenderness and finally sleep.

The grey dawn seeped through the venetian blinds. John woke fifteen minutes before the alarm was set to go off. He lay on his side and watched Illanna, dispassionately now, as she slept. She had the gypsy look, sharp-featured, even in repose. Dark ringlets framed her pale face. He could describe every aspect of that face, but most people when they remembered her remembered the piercing black eyes closed now in sleep. Her body was almost too classically perfect to be sensual. Her wells of passion, however, were such that they often frightened John. Apart from his relationship with her, his life was one of tight control. Physically and mentally, he systematized and controlled until regimentation was automatic. Gypsy was born on the wind.   She was one of the few people he had met whose behavior John could not predict with some reliability. She acted on premises that he could neither understand nor accept. Their relationship was alternately concentric and tangential. She seemed to be pulled into the vortex of John's conventionality only to fly off into a world where he could not follow.

She sighed softly, opening her eyes slowly, incomprehension turning to joy as she recognized where she was and saw John looking at her. She slid over to him and nestled against his broad chest. "Good morning," smiled John. He had a thousand questions but waited for her to speak.

"Do you have to go right away?"

"No. It's early and I don't have to be in before the third shift leaves today."

"I know I said I wasn't coming back, but I had to."

"I'm glad you're back."

"It's not fair to you, John, for me to keep coming and going."

"It was my fault . . ." John began but she put her hand to his mouth.

"It's nobody's fault, John. We think so differently, but it doesn't change the way we feel about each other . . . does it?"

"No. It doesn't."

In the darkened room, John felt removed in time and space from the reality of his world and drawn into the unreality of hers. It didn't frighten him now, because this was the quiet warm part.

"How are things going at the hospital?" There was a sharpness in the question that sent a sudden chill through John.

"What do you mean?"

"Is the Crab still head of Geriatrics?"

"No."

"Where is he?"

"Dead."

"Oh, my God." A look of terror spread across Illanna's face.

"Why? . . . what's the matter?" John was becoming more and more alarmed.

"I killed him!"

"D . . . d . . . don't be ridiculous," stammered John. "We don't even know how . . ." his voice trailed off. "How did you know he was killed?"

"I didn't mean to." Illanna was pleading for forgiveness not from John, but from that other world that frightened him. "When I left I knew you were having trouble with him."

"Yes?"

"Well, you made fun of me when I cast a spell to bring you luck."

John remembered well the argument that had sent her off. His scientific bent had gotten the better of him, and he had mocked her and the basis of what he considered a delusional system.

"I remember."

"I was so mad I decided to prove my power."

"How?"

"I cast a spell against him."

"What kind of spell?"

"That's just it, John, I burned black candles."

John was silent.

"I've never done any black magic before. I didn't mean for him to be hurt, I just wanted him out of the way. Out of *your* way."

A flight of emotions swept through John. He was relieved that this was the extent of her guilt, angry at the black magic mumbo-jumbo, and amused at the nature of her sin and the depth of her belief. He knew better than to show the anger or the amusement. "That was months ago. You can't blame yourself. Someone very real is behind his death. By the way, how did you know something had happened to him just now?"

"The night before last I dreamed about him. It was a weird dream. He was some kind of medieval judge. I was on trial, and he condemned me to death, but I burned black candles against him and he died instead of me. When I woke up I was certain he was dead."

"But that was before he was killed."

Illanna shrugged.

"Well, anyway, now that you're back, maybe you can help me."

"How can I help?"

"The person who killed Azahdi may be someone calling himself 'Malleus Maleficarum.'" Illanna gasped at the forbidden name. John explained about the note and Dr. Johnson's assignment. "I don't know anyone who knows more about witchcraft than you. You can help me interpret that aspect of the note and any other notes we may get."

"I can help more than that."

"How?"

"I can tell if you are actually looking for a witch or only someone using the language."

John fought down his skepticism. "How would you go about it?"

"If someone is using witchcraft against anyone at the hospital, I will be able to feel it." John was silent. "I know you don't believe in any of this, John, but you know what I can do."

John had to grudgingly admit that the Gypsy's power of prediction was uncanny, frightening even. Her dream about the Crab was just the latest in a long string of examples of extrasensory perception she had exhibited since John had known her. John could accept this only in the context of Parapsychology, not in terms of witchcraft and magic. John gave in. "Okay. How can I help?"

"I need something from the hospital." John cast his eyes around the room and then remembered his keys.

"How about these?"

"Perfect . . . but I only need one." Illanna touched one after another until she came to the big jailor's key that opened the front door of Geriatrics. "This one."

"Why?"

Illanna looked at him. "This one links you and the Crab and the hospital."

John started. It *was* the main key he and Azahdi had in common. The keys for meal rooms, examining rooms, offices, etc., were different for staff in different areas but this key was universally held. It opened all of the main entrances and most of the older wards. "You're right," admitted John. He took the key off the ring and handed it to her. Illanna sat cross-legged in front of the window. Lines of light filtered through the venetian blinds, illuminating bands of milky white skin. She closed her eyes and began to rock back and forth, holding the key with both hands between her breasts.

John watched, fascinated. At first, Illanna was perfectly relaxed, but then a stiffness of her body showed the increased tension. She began to hum a strange tune, the tones of which had not been used since the time of Gregorian chants. John began to get the feeling he always got around her when she was doing "her thing." It wasn't she who was bizarre. The room around her seemed to change, to become ancient and occult. She fitted perfectly, and it was John who felt ill at ease and out of place and time.

Gradually she came out of the trance. At last, John felt he could speak. "Well?"

"It's very strange, John."

"What is?"

"There is so much!"

"So much what?"

"Witchcraft."

"How do you mean?"

"Well, first of all, there are both male and female witches involved."

"Yes?"

"Yes, more than two, and some of them are dangerous."

"In what way?"

"There is both black and white magic going on and some very powerful witchcraft -- far more powerful than anything I have come across. It's so confusing. There is so much."

John shook his head in bewilderment. How could he be listening to this? And yet he knew there was something . . . something. "Will you come to the hospital with me?"

"No."

John remembered the hearing. "You're right, it's too dangerous. What are you going to do?"

"Do you have a copy of <u>The Malleus Maleficarum</u>?"

"No. I have excerpts and commentaries on it in some of my abnormal psychology tests."

"Well, I can probably get my hands on a copy today. I have to close up the shop, too."

"I'm going to start going through the records of the hospital and see if I can get a line on Malleus that way."

Illanna shook her head. "I think patients are involved, but not directly. One of the things that is so confusing is that some of the witchcraft is demented."

John burst into laughter. "Some of it?!"

Illanna gave him a reproachful look. "John, I'm serious. Some of the feelings I got were not what I expected. I know the feelings of power coming from someone who is practicing witchcraft, but some of the feelings I got were twisted . . . demented. But these were not the powerful ones. The powerful ones were clear and frightening."

II

John sat at the small desk in the main
nursing station of the Psychiatric Treatment
Center. He concentrated on the social history
and psychodiagnostic sections of the records.
These sections had more direct quotes from
the patients. There were a prize lot of
paranoids.

"The sewing machine operators are taking it
all apart. Every night they unstick it and
inject their needles into people while they are
asleep. The babies are all theirs."

"My brother, the president, has assigned me to
run this hospital. If you do not show me
more respect, I will have you fired."

"I am older than time. Three times nine are
the number of men. I read about it in the New
York Times."

All very interesting, but no sign of Malleus.
John found several references to the Devil and
wrote down the case numbers, but saw no
direct connection to witchcraft, much less
Malleus. He broke for lunch and went
downtown to The Grotto. Illanna was already
sitting in a booth at the back of the dimly lit
café. John groped his way to the back, his
eyes still blinded from the bright morning
sunshine. "Hi." John eased himself into the
booth.

"Any luck?" asked Illanna.

John shook his head. "How about you?"

Illanna produced a paperback edition of <u>The Malleus Maleficarum</u>. "It's the 1971 Dover reprint of Radker's 1928 edition."

John picked it up. It seemed innocuous enough. Hard to believe that over a quarter of a million people had been tortured and burned at the stake or hanged because of this scholarly treatise. "It's a shame, in a way, that you could get a copy so easily."

"Why?" A puzzled look creased Illanna's brow.

John was thinking like a policeman. "If our Malleus has a copy, he had to get it somewhere. If it were rare he would have to order it, and the book store would have a record of the order."

Illanna frowned but then brightened. "This edition just came out. All of the other editions are quite rare . . . some extremely rare. So you think that Malleus just purchased the book?"

"No, it's not likely. Paranoid systems take time to develop, and, if this one is centered around the book, Malleus must have had it for some time. On the other hand, he may have had it for a very long time and simply found it at some local book store. I don't think it's worth our while to do that kind of leg work. We will leave that up to Schneider."

"Schneider?"

"May I join you?"

They both looked startled. Schneider was standing over them. John laughed nervously. "We were just talking about you."

"I heard."

"Illanna, I'd like you to meet Detective Schneider. He's in charge of the investigation of Dr. Azahdi's death."

"How do you do . . . miss?"

"Romanowsky . . . Illanna Romanowsky."

Schneider pulled a chair up to the end of the table and sat down. His eyes rested on the book. "Is that it?"

"Yes."

"Where did you get it?"

"Illanna just bought it this morning."

Schneider raised his eyebrows.

"Oh, come now, Schneider, she probably still has the sales slip." Illanna reached for her handbag.

"Never mind," said Schneider. "I would have thought you had a copy already. You seem to know a good deal about it."

"I have read excerpts and descriptions of its significance for psychiatry, but I've never seen an actual copy. Except for this recent edition, Illanna tells me the book is quite rare."

Schneider didn't look convinced, but turned to Illanna. "What's your connection with the case?"

"My connection is not with the case; it's with John. Not that it's any of your business." Illanna was visibly angry over Schneider's manner. Schneider had long been inured to this type of resistance. John watched the interplay with an increasing amusement.

"What do you do for a living?" asked Schneider.

"I'm a witch."

Schneider started. John laughed. "Got you!"

"Miss, if I were you, I wouldn't be quite so flippant. This is serious business."

"But I am serious, I *am* a witch. Ask John."

Schneider turned to the psychologist.

"She's quite right. I used to try to convince her to the contrary, but I'm afraid I failed miserably."

"But you don't believe in witchcraft?"

"I have learned, with some difficulty, to keep an open mind on the subject."

Schneider shook his head. "I was beginning to have considerable respect for you as a scientist . . . but this!"

Now John's anger, which always seemed to surface when Schneider was around, began to return. "Look Schneider, I don't personally give a damn whether you respect me as a scientist or anything else. I didn't invite you here . . . by the way, how did you get here? Illanna didn't conjure you up, because she didn't even know of your existence until a minute ago."

"The nurse told me you usually ate lunch here when you weren't running."

"Well, I planned on having a quiet lunch with my friend. If you wish to join us, you are welcome, but she has nothing to do with the hospital or the case, and I don't like this third degree routine."

"I'm sorry. It's my job." Schneider got up and stalked out of the restaurant.

Illanna looked after the retreating detective. "He's certainly uptight."

"It seems to be his character, but there is more to it than that. Something about the hospital is bugging him; I don't know what."

"He suspects you, doesn't he, John?"

"Yes. The circumstances don't look too good for me." John related the events surrounding Azahdi's death.

The worried look deepened on Illanna's face. "Even so, he can't seriously think you murdered the Crab."

"I don't know, but the latest interchange didn't help matters. We have the book and you didn't exactly put him off the track."

"I'm sorry, John!"

John laughed. "Don't be. I wouldn't have missed that look of his for the world. But seriously, I wouldn't be so outspoken about your profession. You know the problems you had before."

Illanna nodded. "I know, but why can't people just let me be?"

"Most people live in a tight rational world. Anything outside that world is a threat and frightens them."

"What did he want anyway?"

"He never got around to it, did he? I guess your witchcraft spiel confused him, and then I just about asked him to leave. Well, if it's important, he'll get around to it. I'm afraid I'm going to see plenty of him before this is all over."

Illanna and John finished their lunch, talking happily as if they had never been apart. John left the tip and walked up to the front register.

"I'll see you tonight," said John.

III

On the way back to the hospital, John's mind went back over Illanna's case. She was never really a "case" to him when she was around, but when she wasn't he couldn't help slipping into his clinical mode. He could never sort out whether she was one of his most spectacular successes or devastating defeats. Nor could he tell if there was anything now, or if there ever had been anything wrong with her in the first place.

There was no question in his mind that the commitment hearing had been a railroad job engineered by the landlord, but, by any normal standards, she did have a full-blown delusional system. The sticking point was that John was less and less convinced as time went on that Illanna was delusional. She clearly believed she was a witch. There were no emotional or behavioral consequences of this belief which would have caused her problems, except for the fear she engendered in other people. The fear grew out of the very acceptance of the fact that she was a witch.

John could well imagine, in a time when the world was ruled by superstition, why some people feared witchcraft and witches. That same primordial fear appeared even today in the so-called "modern world."

In any event, John had not been able to "cure" her of the belief and had gotten her out of the hospital illegally . . . if Schneider ever tumbled onto that! His beloved witch! For himself, he would change nothing about her now, but he was afraid for her in a world of non-acceptance. And now, with this business at the hospital, would she be pulled into the mess? Thank God, Schneider hadn't seemed to believe her when she said she was a witch.

John remembered the first time he talked to Illanna . . . interviewed her really. After the hearing, he had asked Johnson about her, and the Superintendent suggested that he do the psychological work-up on her.

She sat huddled on a bench in the corner of the locked admission ward of the Psychiatric Treatment Center. She was obviously terrified, which didn't surprise John, because many of the new admissions were frightened. But she was one of the unfortunate patients who was not terrified of hallucinations from their own secret world. She was terrified of the ward itself and of the other patients.

"Miss Romanowsky?"

"Yes?" She latched onto the normal face like a drowning man latches onto a life preserver.

"I'm Dr. John Lowell. I would like to talk with you for a few minutes, if I may."

"Certainly."

"How are things going?"

She looked at him incredulously. "How are things going? How do you think they are going in this crazy place? Weren't you at the trial?"

"Hearing," John corrected.

"Hearing to you. I was on trial."

John observed with some satisfaction that the fear was rapidly changing to anger. "I was at the hearing."

"Do you think I'm insane?"

"The term insanity has very little relevance for our work here."

"Well, it has a helluva lot of relevance to my being here. Cut out the Rogerian echo-talk and answer me."

John laughed out loud. "What do you know about Rogers?"

It was Illanna's turn to laugh. "What is it they say? I'm in here for being crazy, not for being stupid."

The laughter was even better than the anger.

"Well, whatever approach I use, and you may choose the one you prefer, I am here to help you all I can."

"The only way you can help is to get me out of this place before I really do go crazy."

"I can't get you out until I know something about you."

"What do you want to know?"

"Well, first, why do you think you are in here?"

"Because I wouldn't sleep with my landlord."

John had asked that question a thousand times and had heard many different answers, but this was a new one. "Would you care to explain that?"

"Yes . . . Rogers."

"No . . . I really don't understand and would like to."

"Okay. You heard Kilpatrick at the tri . . . hearing?"

"Yes."

"He said that I practiced witchcraft in the backyard."

"I remember."

"How did he know that?"

"He didn't say."

"He knew it because he's a God damn peeping Tom."

"*What?*"

"Do you know anything at all about witchcraft rituals?"

"Very little."

"Well, many of the rituals are performed naked. The apartments all have fenced in yards which provide complete privacy, but apparently Kilpatrick took his handy dandy peephole maker and cut himself in on the action. He figured if I was running around the yard naked, I must be an easy lay. When he got enough nerve to come around to the front door, I called him an old letch and told him I'd call the police if he spied on me again. He said he'd take action, and he certainly did!"

"I am willing to accept the fact that your landlord's motives may not have been of the purest, but it was not his description of your activities which got you in here."

"What then?"

"You claimed to be a witch!"

"I don't claim to be a witch. I am a witch. Why shouldn't I be?"

"Witchcraft is something outside of the experience of most people, certainly the Judge at the hearing."

Illanna studied the psychologist for a moment and then asked, "What is a witch?"

John shrugged. "I don't know."

"By definition, a witch is someone who practices witchcraft. I practice witchcraft, and therefore I am a witch. Q.E.D."

"Syllogistic logic aside, it is your belief in witchcraft which the Judge considered delus . . . illogical."

"I'm not afraid of the word delusional Doctor, even if you are. I'm not delusional."

"Well, that is certainly the bone of contention."

"If I can prove to you that I am not delusional, you will get me out of here?"

"Well, it would certainly help."

"Don't fence with me. If I am not delusional, I am not crazy, and if I am not crazy, I shouldn't be in here. Right?"

John took the plunge. "Right."

"Okay. What is a delusion?"

John recited the classic psychiatric definition. "A delusion is a false belief, maintained despite experiences and evidences to the contrary."

"In what way am I deluded?"

"Because you believe you are . . ," John sidestepped the logical trap. "You believe in witchcraft."

"What evidence do you need?"

John was stumped. "I guess I don't know very much about witchcraft. What do witches do?"

"There are many misconceptions, but the one thing most people usually associate with us, and which is essentially correct, is that we work spells."

"What sort of spells?"

"To get what we or someone else wants -- the return of a lover, money, a favorable business transaction, etc."

"And people come to you for that?"

"Yes."

"What else?"

"Prophesy."

"What kind?"

"I just can't get you off Rogers, can I?"

"Ms. Romanowsky, it's the most comfortable way for me to communicate, and your analysis of my style is not helping that process."

"Okay. I'm sorry, but if you really want to communicate, you can cut the Ms. Romanowsky routine and call me Illanna."

"It's a deal, and you can call me John."

"All right, John. There are several methods of prophesy used by witches, depending upon their talents and philosophical leanings. The more common ones are palmistry, card reading, crystal gazing, astrology and reading tea leaves.”

“What else?”

“Divination.”

“Divination?”

Illanna grimaced, but continued. “Finding things.”

John suddenly had an inspiration. “Can you find things for other people?”

“Certainly.”

John pushed the call button to the nursing station. “Cathy?”

“Yes, Doctor?”

“Can you come here a minute?”

The door to the glass enclosure at the end of the ward opened, and a nurse in a white uniform hurried toward them. “Is something wrong?”

“No, everything is fine. Didn’t you tell me the other day that you lost your keys?”

“Yes.”

“Have you found them yet?”

“No, and I’ve looked everywhere. If I don’t find them by tomorrow, I have to pay for new ones and the fine!”

"Illanna here says she can help people find things. Will you help her?" he said, turning back to Illanna.

"If I can."

The nurse looked puzzled. John turned to Illanna again. "What do you need?"

"A piece of unused paper, a blue pen and a description of the keys."

John rummaged through his jacket and came up with a note pad and a pen.

"Will this do?"

"Fine."

Illanna looked up at the nurse. Cathy was still perplexed, but described the keys. "There were eight keys in a brown snap-shut case."

Illanna drew a picture of the case on the note pad, tore the top sheet off, folded it carefully four times, and handed it to the nurse. "Put this in your left hand pocket and don't look at it. If at any time you feel like looking for the keys, do it . . . even if you feel it is useless or an unlikely place for the keys to be. Otherwise, just put them out of your mind for now."

The nurse turned toward the nurse's station and then turned back briefly. "Thank you . . . I guess."

John laughed. "Well, if nothing else, that will give her something to talk about."

"Are you testing me?" Illanna asked seriously.

"Not you," said John. "Divination."

"Well, it's not a good test. Just because I can't help her doesn't mean divination doesn't exist."

"Proving the null hypothesis." John muttered under his breath.

"Exactly."

John started out of his professional reserve. "What?"

"You can't prove the null hypothesis," said Illanna.

"Rogers is one thing," said John. "Any omnivorous reader could have come across him, but inferential statistics is quite another matter. Where did you pick that up?"

"I was an anthropology major at Bryn Mawr and had a number of Psych courses, including Experimental and Statistics."

John whistled. "This is going to be more difficult than I thought."

"What is?"

"Having to convince you that such things do not exist."

"It's going to be damn near impossible . . . I might end up convincing you that they do exist."

"Well, you said you couldn't help her."

"No, I didn't. I said *if* I couldn't, it doesn't prove anything. She'll find her keys alright."

John was on firmer ground now. This confidence in the face of a very iffy situation was more like the delusions he was used to. He smiled condescendingly.

Illanna picked up his change in manner even before he could reply. "I don't have to prove anything to you, but wait and see."

John was uncomfortable again and terminated the interview as quickly as possible, promising to drop in on her the next morning.

IV

The next morning came soon enough. As he passed the nurse's station, Cathy rapped on the glass motioning him to come in. "John, I found them!"

"Where?"

"In the basement of my house. Remember I told you my husband has been working down there finishing it for a rec room?"

"Yes."

"Well, I didn't remember being down there, but last night, while I was watching television, I got the urge to go down to see how he was doing. When I got down there, I saw the big overstuffed chair we were going to throw out and sat down in it to watch him work. As soon as I sat down, I remembered I had done the same thing last week, and it occurred to me that maybe the keys had fallen out of my pocket. I looked under the cushion and there they were."

"Well, that's all very well," mused John, "but that doesn't prove anything."

"But, John, look what she gave me."

Cathy showed John the paper Illanna had given her. It was a fairly good drawing of a case with keys in it.

"So?"

"How many keys did I tell her were in the case?"

John thought back. "Eight."

"She only drew six."

John shrugged. "Maybe that's all she could fit into the drawing."

"But, John . . . look!" Cathy held out the case and John saw the six keys. Cathy muttered, "It's crazy."

"It's all just a coincidence," said John, but he didn't sound as sure of himself. He started down the ward and quickened his pace when he saw Illanna huddled in the corner. The day before Illanna had looked frightened. Now she looked terrified.

"Wha . . . what's the matter?" stammered John.

"Get out of here!" screamed Illanna.

John backed off and sat down at the other end of the bench. After a moment, John said quietly, "Let me help you."

Illanna put her hands over her face and began to sob. "No one can help me."

"I can try." He slid down next to her and suddenly Illanna was against him sobbing into his broad shoulder. John put his arm around her and held her gently. "Now . . . tell me about it."

"Last night an aide tried to rape me."

John's hand gripped involuntarily on her shoulder and Illanna winced. "I'm sorry," said John, relaxing, "which aide?"

"I don't know his name . . . the big redhead."

John didn't know the aides on the second and third shifts on this ward. "I'll go find out."

"No! Don't leave!" Illanna looked pleadingly at John.

"Do you want to talk about it?"

"I can't, John, I'm so scared. I can't get out, and he said he'd be back tomorr . . . today." She shuddered.

"That you don't have to worry about. He won't be back until we get this straightened out."

"What can you do?"

"First, find out who he is, and then get the Superintendent to keep him off this ward until this is dealt with."

"You do believe me, John?"

"I have no reason not to."

"But you didn't believe any of the things I told you yesterday."

"No, but I believe you believe them, so you are not lying to me. The ultimate truth of anything is somewhat problematic, but it's easier separating people who tell the truth as they know it from the liars. I don't think you are a liar. If you were, you wouldn't be in here."

"What do you mean?"

"You are intelligent enough to have denied you were a witch at the hearing. That's all it would have taken to get you off the hook. I really wish you had."

"If I had known all this would happen, I probably would have, but I'm so tired of trying to appear like everybody else . . . I'm not."

"No, you're not."

John left, promising to come back after he talked to Dr. Johnson. He stopped briefly at the desk to find out who had been on duty the night before and quickly identified an aide who fit the description Illanna had given. Armed with this information, he crossed the street to the Administration Building.

Peggy sat doing her nails and, seeing it was John, didn't move to hide the paraphernalia.

"I have to see Dr. Johnson."

"He's in conference with some biggie from downtown."

"I don't care. This is an emergency and can't wait."

Peggy pushed the intercom button. "Excuse me, Doctor, but Dr. Lowell needs to speak to you . . . it's an emergency."

"I'll see him in my old office."

Peggy motioned John down the hall to a small door almost completely hidden behind a tall planter. John walked in a second before Johnson slipped into the room.

"What is it?" Johnson looked peeved.

"I think we have an attempted rape of a female patient by a male staff."

"Can't you deal with it?"

"I want to keep the aide off the ward until I check into it. I need your authority to move or suspend him."

"I can't do that, John. You know the union will yell bloody murder."

"Well, then, let me move her to another ward."

"Is she on a locked ward?"

"Yes."

Johnson checked through the census cards on his desk. "We have no female beds on locked wards except the Admission Ward."

"That's where she is now."

"Then I don't see what we can do."

"We have to do something."

Johnson kept looking at the door adjoining his old office with the new one. "John, I can't be bothered with this now. I have the Deputy Secretary in there."

"Will you call me after the meeting?"

"Yes."

John paced up and down the empty office for a couple of minutes, his feelings of frustration increasing. He had to resolve this today. He went back to the Admission Ward, stopping at the nursing office.

"Cathy. When is Rick coming on duty?"

"Third shift . . . eleven o'clock."

John walked to the back of the ward where Illanna was still huddled at the end of the bench. She looked up expectantly. "It's all set," John lied. "Either you or he will be moved before tonight."

"Which?"

"We haven't worked out the details yet, but I have the Superintendent's assurance that it will be resolved today."

Illanna searched his face and didn't seem reassured, but said, "Okay."

John walked back to his office in Geriatrics to wait for Dr. Johnson's call.   It never came. By three o'clock, panic started to set in and he called, only to be told by Peggy that the superintendent was gone for the day.

John was immobilized; his mind kept churning over the horrible possibilities . . . his promise to Illanna . . . his impotence to protect her. By four o'clock, he had decided.

V

There was no moon. The back of the hospital
was all woodland. John pulled his Jaguar
behind a picnic pavilion. Security would never
see it, unless they got out of the patrol car and
walked behind the cooking shed. John knew
that was unlikely with two hundred acres to
patrol and one car. He crept from building to
building, keeping the monoliths between
himself and the street lights. He was fairly
certain that no one had seen him when he got
to the fire exit of the Psychiatric Treatment
Building. He slipped through the fire door and
ascended the tower to the third floor. He
checked his watch. Five minutes to eleven.
He was counting on the ward routine to be the
same here as it was in Geriatrics. "The
changing of the guard" should occupy all staff
at the other end of the ward. With only the
low night lights on, this end should be in
almost total darkness. He took a deep breath,
unlocked the fire exit door, and went in. The
exit was in a cul-de-sac at the end of the ward.
He looked around the corner and saw that no
staff were on the ward. At the far end, both
shifts were huddled in the nurse's office.
Fortunately, Illanna's room was closest to the
exit. He flattened himself against the wall,
sliding the last five feet, and went in. He
heard a gasp behind him and, swinging
around, sharply saw Illanna with a chair

raised over her head. He caught it as she almost dropped it on him.

"John!"

"Shhh!"

"Oh God, I thought you'd left me."

"Quiet," John whispered. "Let's go."

"My things."

"No time."

John pulled her through the door, and they crept around the corner. John listened . . . nothing from the other end of the ward.

"We have to hurry. They'll be checking beds as soon as they come on duty."

They flew down the steps and darted from building to building, retracing the route John had taken. They had to get out before security was notified that she was missing.

The last building before the woods was the Geriatrics Ward. As they stood in the shadow of a corner, John heard the page.

"Illanna Romanowsky return to your ward, Illanna Romanowsky return to your ward, Illanna . . ."

He pulled her across the narrow strip of light from the window and into the wooded area. Branches whipped John's face as he lumbered through the underbrush in the general direction of his car. When they broke into the clearing, they were only a few feet from where he had parked. His wheels spun through the gravel, and then squealed as they hit the pavement on the back road. In his mirror, he saw the flashing blue light of the security car. His lights were still off, and he fought to stay on the back road he could barely see. He switched on the headlights as he pulled out of the back gate. No car lights showed behind him. Security must have continued their loop. Thank God. There were not too many cars like John's around, and they would have remembered it if they had seen it. He probably could have explained why he was on the grounds, but someone might put two and two together.

He felt Illanna's eyes on him, but he didn't look over.

"Why did you do it, John?"

"There didn't seem to be any other way. You didn't belong in there, and I couldn't keep the aide out."

"Won't you get in trouble?"

"Not if they don't find out."

"Where are we going now?"

"Where do you want to go?"

"I can't go back to the apartment. I don't even know what they did with my things."

"Well, you can stay at my place tonight."

Illanna didn't answer.

"You can trust me," he said gently.

"I know that, John."

CHAPTER FOUR -- RASPUTIN

I

The small group fidgeted, each member working out his or her individual anxiety with an individual tic. The plump blond tugged nervously at her sleeve, the cadaverous young man looked at the door every few seconds and the matronly woman at the end of the table hyperventilated. Fortunado was late. He was always late but insisted that his staff be punctual. It was only one facet of a multiple-faceted campaign to intimidate his subordinates. From the reactions around the table, the campaign was succeeding admirably.

At ten minutes after one, Fortunado came out of his office into the adjoining conference room. Richard Fortunado, D.S.W., Director of Social Services, had the hospital nickname of Rasputin. He looked the part. His long curly black hair merged into his full beard. Piercing black eyes glared out from the tangled mass. A glint of cruelty or madness or both played in their depths. He had developed his disheveled appearance carefully in graduate school and was able to maintain it in this backwash of the State system. The Rasputin parallel was not just appearance deep. He had power. One felt drawn into the dark, hypnotic eyes. Primitive feelings of savagery and cruelty emanated from him. Few people who met him were not shaken by the experience. Yet he was in a "helping profession". The apparent paradox of his role in social service versus his personality did not occur to most people who were confronted by so many paradoxes in the State Mental Health System. His competence in dealing with the myriad of State and Federal laws and regulations and his dominance over his staff left very little room for attack. There were multiple rumors about him, perpetuated by his lack of communication concerning his personal life. One of the most persistent was that he had a history of mental illness himself.   Like all of the others, however, no one knew for sure.

The group stopped fidgeting at his entrance and held rigid expressions, then smiled as he took his place at the head of the long table. He shuffled memorandums, sorting them in terms of relevance and urgency.

"Ahem! Paul!"

Paul jumped. "Y-yes?"

"What have you done about those referrals to the Eddington Boarding Home?"

"I-I'm looking into it."

"What does that mean?"

"We have to make an on-site visit. We've never sent anyone up there before, and we don't know what the place looks like."

"I appreciate that, but we need the beds." Fortunado was scowling at the already shaken young man who was shrinking further into his loose-fitting suit.

Fortunado spread his scowl around the table. "We have got to establish a policy around here. We cannot afford to be so finicky about where we place people. The waiting list is growing every day. The Courts are on our backs, the Base Service Units are on our backs, and now the legislature is getting into the act."

Mrs. Miller spoke up. "The legislature?"

"Yes, apparently the nephew of one of the State Senators was on the waiting list to come in. We had no beds, so the Base Service Unit tried to deal with him on an out-patient basis. He got drunk and tore up a bar. The police jailed him last night. This morning they found him hanging in his cell. Now the Governor is all over us."

"But surely they can't blame the hospital?"

"Can't?" Fortunado laughed. "Who are the legislators going to blame? Themselves for not appropriating the money to get our buildings life-safety-coded? Themselves for swallowing the Radical Psychiatrist line of 'no such thing as mental illness?' Themselves for counting on a community mental health system that has no supervised beds? Themselves for swallowing 'Deinstitutionalization' hook, line and sinker? No—it's either them or us, and they choose us."

Mary Anne looked up from the table which she had been studying intently since Fortunado began his tirade. "What can we do?"

Fortunado sat back and the tension in the room decreased a notch. Now he would tell them what they could do and would do if they knew what was good for them. "For openers we can stop worrying about 'what places look like.'" The thinly veiled sarcasm diminished Paul still further. "If we have a community bed available, we use it."

Mrs. Miller spoke up again. "Beds are not the only issue here. We have a moral obligation to . . .". Her speech trailed off under Fortunado's withering glance.

"Moral obligation my ass. We get an average of ten admissions a week. That's 520 a year, 520 in, 520 out -- that's mathematics. Morality has nothing to do with it."

Mary Anne took her turn. "The whole system seems self-defeating to me. We push them out, but the return rate keeps going up. At first it was just the revolving door phenomenon, but now it seems almost like a juggling act – how many patients can we keep in the air at one time?"

Fortunado's patience was wearing thin. He was not used to this much resistance from his carefully intimidated flock. "Cut the philosophy. Johnson has been ordered by the Deputy Secretary to reduce the waiting list by half within the next month and down to zero by the month after that."

"I bet he loved that. You know how he feels about placing people before they are ready." Mrs. Miller was standing up better than the others, but then she only had two years to go before retirement.

Fortunado's sarcasm was turned on her. "He wasn't *asked* to reduce the waiting list, he was *told* to do it. Now he can either go over the census and violate the life-safety codes, or he can increase placement. He has left the problem in my lap, and we are going to solve it. The first step is to fill Eddington's Boarding home – now, not tomorrow or next week. Is there any further discussion? Okay, I want a list of ten patients ready to go on my desk this afternoon. I'll leave you three to decide where they come from."

Fortunado stomped out of the room, leaving the three of them looking at each other.

II

The tunnels beneath the hospital were rarely used these days. Most of the incidents of rape and violence took place in these catacombs, and patients and staff alike avoided them. In foul weather, groups would use the tunnels between the main buildings, but few people would venture down alone. Some of the old-time nurses and grounds crew had a fair idea of the extent of the labyrinth still in use, and also all of the older buildings which had been empty for years. The tunnel system, like the hospital itself, had developed over more than 100 years -- passages walled up, opened again, new ones built. Nowhere was there a complete record of the system.

Dr. Fortunado stretched in his chair and looked up at the clock.

"Ginny, I'm going out for a while." He switched off the intercom, put on his coat and went out into the hall of the Administration Building. He took the elevator down two flights to the sub-basement, watching intently out of the small window at each floor. No one was standing around or waiting for the elevator. When he stepped out, he looked carefully up and down the musty hallway and then slipped through a door which led to an old hydrotherapy room. Dust and grime covered the white tile floor between rows of tubs. This particular torture chamber had been out of service for many years. Hydrotherapy had given way to more modern electrical techniques. At the back of the room was an iron door with a small slit at eye level. The door was locked with a large hand-wrought padlock which looked as though it hadn't been opened in a hundred years. Fortunado pulled at a chain around his neck and produced a skeleton key. The lock opened meticulously. Careful inspection would have revealed that it was well oiled. Even extreme caution could not avoid thin nicks around the key hole, but nobody came down here except Rasputin.

He swung the heavy door open and stepped into a tomb of silent screams. The brick-lined chamber was barely tall enough to stand up in. A narrow stone bench took up half of the left side of this ancient seclusion room. Iron shackles still hung on the wall to the right. A sane man could be driven insane in such a room. Rasputin felt a surge of power.

A sickly streak of gray light filtered through the narrow slit in the door. At the back of the room, he pressed on a brick just below the rectangle of light. The wall pivoted silently and he stepped into the catacomb.

In a niche to the right, a yellow tallow candle stood in a hand-wrought holder. Fortunado lit the candle and started down the steep decline toward the morgue. This was the first tunnel ever built at the hospital. Originally, it connected the main building, which housed most of the patients, and the first additional building, which had been for extremely disturbed patients. For many years now, the second building had served as the morgue. The morgue was located two hundred yards away from the Administration Building, but it was isolated by a woods and steep slope so that the above-ground access was further from the Administration Building than any other part of the hospital. Only Fortunado knew about this direct route.

As he descended into the blackness, a faint murmur began to drift up out of the inky depths. The murmur grew rhythmically into a chant as he reached the end of the tunnel. Fortunado pressed a worn brick in the center of the wall, and it pivoted silently, opening into a small, circular dungeon.

Crossing to the far wall, he stepped into a curiously shaped cavity and peered through the Cyclopean eye. A scene from Bosch's Garden of Earthly Delights lay before him in the blood red glow of the ruby eye. Naked figures stood inside the devil's pentacle etched deep in the stone floor. Queenie, with a black cape hung around her white shoulders, stalked around the circle flicking the naked buttocks with a cat-o-nine tails and leading the eerie chant.

"Algon, Tetragram, Vaycheon, stimulamaton, ezphares retragrammation olyaram irion estyion existion eryona chera orasym, imozm messias soter Emanuel sabaoth adonay, Te Adoro, et Te invoco. Amen."

Fortunado stepped back into the chamber and quickly undressed, donning a red cape and goat's head, which hung next to the sarcophagus. On either side of the idol, stone caps were set into the wall. Lighting the yellow powder in each and blowing out the candle he stepped back into the idol and swung the hinged front out. The room filled with a choking, yellow, sulfuric smoke. He stepped to the edge of the ring and stood still as the smoke settled to the floor. "Why have you summoned me?"

Queenie spoke. "Oh Lord and master, these supplicants wish to honor you with their bodies and their souls."

"I accept their homage and grant them the fulfillment of their carnal lust."

The orgy began, staff and patients writhing on the floor while Fortunado and Queenie looked on. Later, when the last of the patients had filed out and Queenie had returned, she and Fortunado retired to a couch in the circular dungeon and exhausted their own lust built during the half hour of voyeurism.

Sated, Fortunado began to dress.

"With all these cops around we are going to have to cool it for a while."

Queenie was silent.

"I want you to keep an eye on Lowell. Johnson has him snooping around in the records, and he'll be interviewing patients next. He's good friends with Randy, and Randy might let something slip."

"I can control Randy." Queenie smiled.

"I wouldn't be so confident. You got him by the balls, but he really trusts Lowell."

"I can handle Lowell, too."

"You'd like to."

Queenie stamped her foot. "What is that supposed to mean?"

"You know you have the hots for him and he won't give you a tumble."

Queenie went white with rage, but was afraid to attack Fortunado directly.

"That's ridiculous."

"Well, whatever, but keep an eye on Randy and John, particularly when they are together."

"Okay."

They finished dressing, and Fortunado returned to the Administration Building while Queenie followed the staff and patients' route through several other tunnels to Extended Care.

III

Queenie, Mrs. Rachel Slade, was the Director of the Extended Care Unit. The forty-year-old widow was hanging onto youth and beauty with a tenacity which was at least neurotic. John called it the "mirror, mirror on the wall syndrome." Unfortunately, this had gotten back to her. Her feelings toward the psychologist were unbearably ambivalent. She viewed him as a sexual challenge, a trophy to hang with the legion of conquests she had inside and outside of the hospital. She hated him for understanding her vanity and the weakness behind it. She didn't have to be told to keep an eye on John. Lowell-watching was one of her chief activities. She would watch him and have him and then destroy him as she had done with many others. Most of the others she had cast aside out of boredom, but with John, she would possess him only for the purpose of casting him aside. She smiled in anticipation of her triumph.

Rachel was a beautiful woman, short, with a tendency toward plumpness which she successfully fought with a constant diet. Her hair was too black to be natural at her age. She dressed in fashions which would not have stood out in New York, but which set her apart in Lancaster. Her husband's untimely death had left her almost independently wealthy so that she probably would not have had to work, but her extravagant life style required two incomes.

Vanity was at the heart of her system, and man after man played into it and supported it. Just when she began to lose the inevitable battle with age, and self-doubts began to gnaw at her, she came up against John's indifference -- all the more maddening because John didn't even seem to know he was indifferent.

Rachel peeked around the linen case which hid the entrance to the tunnel. This tunnel was not as well concealed and not as unknown as the one used by Fortunado, but then there was the other tunnel which had to be negotiated before reaching the morgue. Queenie had the patients and staff blindfolded before taking them through the concealed door to the last tunnel.

There was no one in the linen room, and she stepped confidently into the hall, taking the elevator to the first floor. Her secretary was sitting at her desk watching the clock as she came in.

"How was it?"

Queenie started and then quickly composed herself as she remembered she had told her she had a luncheon committee meeting with the Mental Health Association.

"Not bad. . . boring."

"You must get tired of meetings."

"That depends on the meeting." Queenie smiled to herself and stepped into her office.

She looked at the mass of memos, computer printouts, census cards, and correspondence Francine had piled on her desk while she was out. She pushed the junk aside irritably and pressed the intercom button.

"Francine?"

"Yes?"

"Call the first floor and see if Randy is up there. If he is, have them send him down." Rachel drummed her fingers on the blotter, staring at the intercom.

"He's coming right down."

Randy sidled through the door moments later.

"Shut the door."

Randy complied and turned toward her with his lopsided grin. He shifted his enormous weight from foot to foot, watching her anxiously.

"Sit down, Randy."

Randy sat down on the short couch which accommodated him about as well as an easy chair did most people.

"I want to talk to you about Dr. Lowell."

A puzzled look came over Randy's face. Staff didn't talk to patients much, and when they did, it was always "How are you doing?" "How's it going?" and the like. Even John didn't talk to him about other staff.

"What?"

"You and Dr. Lowell are pretty close, aren't you?"

"He's my best friend." My only friend, Randy admitted to himself.

"You don't want him to get into trouble, do you?"

"No." The worry lines increased on Randy's brow.

"You know the game we play is against hospital rules."

"Yes." Randy was confused by Mrs. Slade's use of the term "game." He was only dimly aware of the nature of what they did beyond the fact that it was secret and that he enjoyed it. It did not fit into his concept of games, but he accepted anything Mrs. Slade said.

"Dr. Lowell has been asking questions. Has he asked you anything about the devil or witchcraft?"

"No."

"Well, if he does, what are you going to say to him?"

"Nothing."

"Randy, I know you mean that. You don't want him to get into any trouble or the other patients or yourself."

"No."

"I can't stress the importance of this too much, Randy. Not only will it be the end of the game if Dr. Lowell finds out, but he will get into trouble."

"Why?" Randy was struggling to understand what Mrs. Slade was saying.

"Because he is your friend, and everyone will think that he is involved."

Randy shook his head in bewilderment. "But he doesn't . . ." his voice trailed off in confusion.

"Randy, you must trust me. Be on your guard every minute when Dr. Lowell is around."

Bad feelings began to well up in Randy. Their secret had always brought a kind of pleasure to him. That he had been chosen by a beautiful woman like Mrs. Slade from so many patients had made him feel special. Now he had to lie to his friend to keep him from getting into trouble. Randy shook his head. "I won't say anything, honest."

"I know you won't Randy. Please tell me if Dr. Lowell asks you anything."

"I will."

Randy left the office feeling more depressed than he had in months. With the depression came a growing fear that he would do something to harm Mrs. Slade or Dr. John.

Rachel was pleased with herself. It was clear that she had absolute control over Randy, and now she also had a spy in the enemy camp. She knew that Randy would faithfully report anything he found out about John's investigation. Randy saw him every day, so she could comply with Fortunado's mandate and pursue her own game at the same time.

IV

Over in Geriatrics, the afternoon team meeting was convening. John was a little disorganized. Since Azahdi's death, he was the team leader. This was okay, because he had always been the informal leader even when Azahdi had been on the team. His research into the patients' records, however, had left him no time to review the progress notes before meeting with the team about this month's patients.

He glanced around the table . . . everyone present: Paul, the case manager, looking more nervous than usual if that was possible; Judy, the charge nurse, pleasant as always; John Davis, from Activities; and Ted, the new aide. John wrote down the date and members of the team present.

"Who's up?" John looked at Judy.

"We have five today, but Paul said he had something important to discuss first."

"Well?" John turned to Paul.

"Dr. Fortunado needs a list of 10 patients to go to Eddington's Boarding Home this afternoon."

"We don't have 10 patients ready for placement in the whole unit, and we certainly don't have 10 from the County."

"We . . . we . . . we're not supposed to worry about County of origin. This is an emergency."

John raised his eyebrows. "What kind of emergency?"

"The Governor told Dr. Johnson he had to reduce the waiting list."

"I doubt if the Governor even knows what a waiting list is."

"Well, actually, it was the Deputy Secretary from Central Office, but the Governor is concerned."

"Why?"

"Because the nephew of one of the Senators hanged himself in jail."

"And he was on the waiting list?"

"I guess."

John's puzzlement had turned to irritation during the interview and was progressing toward anger. "We have a formal letter of agreement with all Base Service Units that we will not place patients out of their County of origin. If we suddenly dump ten patients into Lebanon County who are not from Lebanon, you might as well throw those agreements in the trash can."

"B . . . B . . . But, Dr. Fortunado said . . ."

"I don't care what he said; I won't do it. It's a moot point anyway. You know we don't have ten patients in the Unit ready for any type of placement, much less to a boarding home. What is this boarding home like? I don't know anything about it other than it is in Lebanon County.

"Well, it's new."

"New what? New building? New operation?"

"I . . . I . . . don't know. I haven't seen it . . ." Paul's voice trailed off in embarrassment.

John struggled to control himself. He knew it wasn't Paul's fault, but there was no one else to vent his frustration on. "This is unbelievable!! You want a list of ten patients who aren't ready to go, to a County which they don't come from, to be placed in a facility you haven't seen. Get Fortunado over here."

Paul almost ran out of the room. The rest of the team sat in embarrassed silence.

John returned to the business at hand. "Who's first?"

Judy pushed the medical record down the table. "Henry Eshelman."

John smiled. He couldn't be angry and think about Henry at the same time. He flipped through the progress notes. Henry seemed much the same, except for an Unusual

Incident report. Henry had gotten into a fight
with one of the grounds crew, had thrown
him over a hedge and broken his collar bone.
John turned to John Davis. "What about this
fight Henry got into?"

"The grounds crew is pretty upset. They don't
want Henry working with them anymore.
They are afraid of him."

"I can understand that, but what precipitated
the fight?"

"Apparently a new guy didn't want Henry to go
on break because they were right in the
middle of doing something, so he told Henry
he couldn't go. Henry picked him up and
threw him over a hedge. He's hurt pretty
badly and is going to be off work for at least
six weeks."

"Didn't anyone tell him that Henry works
when he wants and when he wants to quit he
quits?"

Davis shrugged.

"The grounds crew doesn't think it's their
responsibility to be bothered with clinical
matters. They treat the patient workers like
staff."

"That's a good general principle, but the
patients are not exactly like staff. Henry isn't
exactly like anybody."

"Well, anyway, they want him off the crew."

"I can't go along with that. The crew was specifically told not to interfere with Henry when he wanted to stop working. His history is very clear, and, after all, the man is eighty years old and doesn't have to work at all if he doesn't want to."

"But the crew is likely to grieve to the union if he comes back."

Dr. John tapped his pen on the desk impatiently. "There are certain risks involved in working around mental patients. We try to minimize those risks by keeping a close eye on unpredictable patients. Henry is predictable and normal as long as you do not interfere with his hospital routine. Tell the crew he is to continue to work and remind them again about his routine."

The door burst open, and Fortunado strode into the room. "Paul tells me you are unwilling to cooperate with Dr. Johnson's order."

John wasn't going to be buffaloed that easily. "Paul didn't say it was an order from Johnson. He said it came from you."

"I'm acting on instructions from the Superintendent."

"Dr. Johnson ordered that ten patients from Geriatrics be placed in a boarding home out of their County of Origin?"

"Not exactly."

"Then what?"

"He said that we had to get the waiting list down by one half by the end of the month."

"But he didn't say how to do it?"

"No. He left it to me."

"Well, I doubt if he is going to allow you to trample all over the letter of agreement we have with Lebanon."

Now Fortunado was on the defensive. "What else can we do?"

"We can use standard placement procedures. The team will provide you with a list of patients ready for placement, with the recommendation of appropriate levels of care and County of origin. Your staff will have to find appropriate beds."

"And if they can't?"

"Then the patients won't get placed."

"But the Secretary . . ."

"Secretary be damned. He's got responsibilities . . . and we have ours. We cannot place our patients in settings which are not appropriate."

"You'll be hearing from Johnson."

"Probably," said John to the closing door. The staff was watching John intently. It was a rare occasion to see Fortunado even resisted, let alone beaten. One of the things which set John apart from the administrative staff was that his actions stemmed from his perception of the clinical needs of the patients, and he couldn't adjust them to political realities. He had survived other wars with the administration because he had an ally in Johnson. The pressure, however, had never come from so high up.

The rest of the team meeting was uneventful except that it ran over the shift change, so Judy had to leave before it was over. John went back to his office. A pile of records was on his desk. He felt like the Sorcerer's Apprentice. Once nursing started delivering the charts, they just kept on coming. His head was swimming from reading the histories. He was becoming convinced that this approach was not going to pay off. If a patient was calling himself Malleus Maleficarum on admission, John surely would have heard about it. He was the acknowledged historian on the staff, and someone would have told him about Malleus or asked him about it. On the other hand, something kept nagging at the back of his mind. Something about witches and devils which he had seen in the records but he couldn't remember where . . . The phone startled him out of his memory probe.

"Geriatrics."

"John?"

"Yes."

"It's Johnson."

Yes, Sir."

"Fortunado's been in here. He's in a rage."

"I'll bet."

"You know he's just trying to help us out of a tough spot."

"I appreciate the dilemma, Doctor, but I can't do what Dick wants without breaking all the rules you yourself laid down."

"I know, John, but we have to do something, the Governor's behind this."

"We *can* do something."

"What?"

"Use the system we have set up, but work a little harder at it. If we document our attempts at placement, Downtown has to be satisfied. Even the Governor can't order us to put patients out on the street. The system is doing plenty of that without our help."

"I know. Every time I go downtown I see former patients hanging around the street corners with their shopping carts. We may not have put them out on the street, but that's where they are now."

John sighed. "We all know the tragedies of deinstitutionalization, but it has had some positive effects. It has put some of the responsibilities for mental health services back on the community where it belongs."

Johnson was silent for a moment. "Well, John, what are we going to do?"

"Send a memo to all the teams. Instruct them to make out a list of the patients in order of placement readiness by level of care and County of origin. Get a list from Fortunado of the social workers with the best relationship with each Base Service Unit, and send them down with the list and see what each County can come up with. We should be able to get enough beds in the next two weeks to reduce the waiting list. The next group is going to be more difficult."

"Okay, John . . . thanks."

John hung up and turned back to the mountain of paper.

V

Illanna parked her van behind the brownstone
building where she had her shop. She
unlocked the paint-chipped door and walked
through the small storage room in the back to
the long store front. The smell of new leather
permeated the room. Handmade bags and
pocketbooks of all descriptions hung from
hooks in the ceiling and lay scattered at
random on low wooden tables. At the front of
the shop were a leather work bench and table
with a cash register by the door. The late
afternoon sun slanted through the plate glass
window, casting long shadows on the stained-
oak flooring. Illanna didn't turn on the light.
She sat with her back to the sun and watched
the deepening red glow playing on the myriad
surfaces. Suddenly she reached in her
handbag and pulled out a deck of cards. She
cut them to the Queen of Spades, shuffled
and cut to the Queen again. Then she started
turning the cards up one by one in rows of
seven. The black Queen came up next to the
Jack of Hearts. She walked to a back table
where an object glowed red with the setting
sun. She gazed for a long time into the crystal
ball.

On the drive back to John's house, Illanna
went through two red lights and a stop sign.
Fortunately, her preoccupation wasn't shared
by the majority of late afternoon commuters,
who steered clear of the psychedelic bus. She
hurried into the house, ran upstairs and
quickly changed into her white robe.
Downstairs at the altar, she lit blue candles
and placed a picture of John in front of them.
She took a small vial of blue powder from her
purse and sprinkled it in a circle around the
picture chanting, "Around you, John, a circle
of blue that no evil power can get through."
Three times she cast the protective spell and
then blew out the candles.

When John came back from the hospital, he
found her sleeping on the couch. He smelled
the acrid smoke from the candles and looking
over at the altar, startled at the sight of his
picture and the blue ring. He sat in the easy
chair for some time studying Illanna until she
stirred and began to wake up.

"Hi."

"How long have you been here?"

"Not long."

"Why didn't you wake me?"

John smiled. "I was admiring your taste in
pictures." He glanced over at the altar.
"What's that all about?"

"I think I know where part of the evil is coming from, and it's working against you."

"Against me?" John was fighting his skepticism again and trying to keep it from showing on his face.

"Who is the dark-haired lady?"

John jumped. "What dark-haired lady?"

"Don't play games with me, John."

Witchcraft aside, jealousy was rising in Illanna's mind and manner.

"Well . . ." John hesitated, "when anyone talks about a dark-haired lady at the hospital they mean Rach . . . Mrs. Slade, the Director of the Long Term Care Center. Why?"

"Before I go into that . . . what is she to you?"

"Nothing."

Anger flashed in Illanna's eyes. "Don't give me that John. You almost jumped out of the chair when I asked about a dark-haired lady. Are you involved with her?"

"No." John's sincerity eased the tension which had been building between them.

"Are you sure there is nothing on your side?"

"Yes. What do you mean by on my side?"

"There is no question she is after you."

"I doubt it." John was hedging. He knew he was innocent, but once aroused, Illanna's jealousy was monumental and had caused problems before when there had been less reason than in this situation.

"Don't be coy, John. You know she is after your bod."

John flushed. "Who have you been talking to?"

"No one."

"Then where are you getting all this nonsense?"

"Nonsense?" Illanna was getting angry again.

"Information," John said more carefully.

"First the cards, and then the crystal."

John sighed but said nothing.

"This is important, John, but before I spend too much energy protecting you from her, I need to know you want to be protected."

This last bit of sarcasm seemed to release Illanna from the tangential issue and John sensed that she was ready to tell him what was going on.

"Queenie has made some overtures but she knows I am not interested," John admitted.

Illanna raised her eyebrows at the nickname Queenie, but kept herself under control. "Okay, I knew she had the hots for you, but I didn't want to interfere with your love life."

John started to protest.

"It's all right. I believe you, John, and anyway, it's really none of my business. I left you, and, even though you look like one, I know you're no monk, so I wouldn't blame you if . . ." Tears welled up in Illanna's eyes and her voice trailed off in confusion.

John pulled her over onto his lap. "I love you, Illanna. There hasn't been anyone since you left, and I have been miserable. Now what is all this about Mrs. Slade?"

Illanna nestled against John's chest and told him about her experiences at the shop.

CHAPTER FIVE -- MOSES

I

"Moses said, 'Let my people go' and the devil rose up and smote him."

Dr. Johnson turned the memorandum over in his hand and pushed the intercom button.

"Peggy?"

"Yes, Doctor."

"Get Lt. Schneider on the phone and then locate Dr. Lowell and have him come over."

Johnson's brow furrowed as he sat staring down at the second missive from Malleus.

"Lt. Schneider's on the line, Doctor."

Johnson picked up the phone. "Schneider?"

"Yes, Dr. Johnson?"

"I've got another note here from Malleus."

"How did you get it?"

"It was on my desk this morning like the other one."

"I'll be right over. Don't handle it."

Ten minutes later Peggy buzzed him. "Dr. Lowell's here."

"Send him in, Peggy."

John sidled through the door. "What's up?"

"Another note from Malleus." Johnson pushed the memo across the desk toward the psychologist. John picked it up automatically.

Johnson cleared his throat. "Damn. Schneider said not to touch it, and here we are tracking it up with our fingerprints. Soon he'll be suspecting us."

"He already suspects me," said John absently.

"I don't think he does really, John. You just happen to be handy."

"No, it's deeper than that. I think if he had a really good motive he'd have me arrested."

"Well, he doesn't."

"Not yet," said John enigmatically.

Johnson was puzzling over this response when Schneider arrived.

"Where's this note?"

Johnson pointed to the memo.

"Did either of you touch it?"

"I'm afraid we both did," Johnson admitted.

Schneider exploded. "Damn it, last time was excusable, but this time you both knew better."

Both Johnson and Lowell dealt with outbursts of anger so often that Schneider barely got a response. "I didn't know what it was until I picked it up, and then I handed it to John. I'm sorry."

Schneider wasn't mollified, but there wasn't anything he could do. He read the note. "Who is this Moses?"

John responded, "As far as I know, it is not one of the hospital nicknames."

Both Schneider and Johnson turned sharply toward John.

"Nicknames?"

John suppressed a smile at the inquiry. "Many people in the hospital, patients and staff, have nicknames."

"I wasn't aware of that," said Dr. Johnson.

"You wouldn't be," said John. "The superintendent is still held in awe around here."

"Then I'm surprised I'm not Moses," chided Johnson.

"Oh no," said John, "you're 'God'."

Schneider choked and Johnson laughed out loud. "You're kidding!"

"No, you've been 'God' ever since I've worked here."

Schneider had himself back under control. "What's yours?"

"I have two that I know of. But you never know the ones they don't use to your face."

"What are they?"

"One's Sugar Bear."

"And the other?"

"Well, you're bound to find out eventually. In the Long Term Center I'm known as 'The Hammer'."

Johnson gasped. "But that's . . ."

"The translation of Malleus," stated John, finishing Johnson's sentence.

The room was silent for what seemed an interminable amount of time. Finally, Schneider spoke. "Why do they call you that?"

"It's a reference to my style of play in the basketball tournaments."

"How so?"

"You have noticed I am not set up ideally for the game. I lack finesse. Some people claim I intentionally run over people. It's a habit I acquired playing football."

"How long have they been calling you this?"

"At least two years that I know of, probably since the first tournament I was in three years ago."

Schneider was wrestling with himself internally. "Dr. Lowell, this is very serious. First you threaten Azahdi, and you were the last person to see him alive. Then you go back to his office when specifically instructed not to do so, and now we find a link between you and the memo writer. I have half a mind to arrest you right now."

John glared at him. "Half a mind won't make it, Schneider. I've already gone over that 'last person to see him alive' routine, and the nickname is a coincidence. I didn't write either of the damn notes. Do I look stupid enough to use a name I know I'm called at the hospital? Anyway, you have no direct connection between Azahdi's death and Malleus."

"There are too many coincidences around here, and they all seem to revolve around you, Dr. Lowell."

"Well, if you're going to arrest me, get it over with or let me go, because I have a conference at 10:00." John looked up at the clock.

"That's right, the Senator is coming down this morning."

"Which Senator?"

"Goldstein." In the excitement of finding the memo and the dramatic interchange between the detective and the psychologist, Johnson had completely forgotten about the morning's presentation at the weekly conference. "And I have to introduce him, so I'm afraid you'll have to excuse both of us."

"When is the conference over?"

"At 11:00."

"I would like to see both of you immediately after . . ."

"Oh, all right." Dr. Johnson sounded uncharacteristically peevish. He was not sure how Goldstein was going to be received by staff. Goldstein had been a long-time critic of the State hospital system, and now, with his nephew committing suicide, he would be looking for a scapegoat.

II

The chapel murmured with the casual conversation of fifty odd staff and an equal number of community representatives. The turnout was double the usual attendance because of the prestige of the speaker. A Senator rated the presence of many petty officials from Central Office, but no one really close to the Governor was present.

Goldstein sat in the front row, his leonine mane brushed back over his seersucker suit jacket. He sat relaxed, as one who was accustomed to being the center of attention. Johnson sat in the seat next to him, a little nervous in the situation. Lowell took his characteristic seat in the back of the auditorium.

Johnson walked to the lectern and began mouthing platitudes " . . . and our distinguished guest today needs no introduction . . . coauthor of the Mental Health Act . . . friend of the mentally disabled . . . the Honorable Senator Robert Goldstein."

"In 1975 we introduced legislation designed to strengthen the community Mental Health system. Frankly, our aim was to close the State hospitals down." An angry murmur sprang up among hospital employees. Johnson began to squirm in his seat. "But I see you are still here." There was some laughter from the community representatives, but most of the staff looked pretty grim. "I personally believe that the mentally disabled can be better served in the community, close to their families and social supports, than they can in large isolated institutions." Several of the staff stood ready to walk out but resumed their seats under the withering gaze of Dr. Johnson. "Saz and others have made a strong case that it is illegal to incarcerate people whose only crime is that they deviate from society's so-called norms." The murmuring was getting ugly, and individual phrases began to be inaudible at the front. Johnson couldn't look everywhere at once. Goldstein was either deaf or could care less, because he continued to plough ahead with the "no such thing as mental illness" dogma which had decimated State hospital systems all over the country. "To restrain and abuse patients for the sake of holding onto your petty jobs. . ." the angry cry was silenced as the lights went out. Somewhere a door slammed, a muffled cry came from the direction of the lectern. A minute later the lights came on and, slumped across the podium with his head turned impossibly toward the ceiling, Goldstein's sightless eyes gazed at the cross over the Chapel stage. Johnson rushed to the lectern, but he knew it was no use before he got there.

There was confusion throughout the auditorium, and another problem soon became evident. Scattered throughout the crowd were a number of patients. A few always wandered in when they saw the doors open. Some probably were aware of the nature of the conference and a very few even the topic to be discussed.

Now, however, the natural crowd hysteria was affecting some of the patients and they began to cry and scream. The disturbance was spreading at an alarming rate and some of the staff and community members were getting caught up in it. Johnson walked quickly to the phone in the corner and called security. He spoke briefly and then returned to the front of the auditorium but avoided the lectern. "Sit down." The firm authoritarian voice cut through the rising crescendo of confusion. "All community people file out quietly, but stay in the area immediately in front of the Chapel – do not leave the area. The police may want to talk to you. Staff, identify the patients from your area and escort each one back to the ward, then return to the Chapel." The specific instructions had a miraculous effect on the situation. In a few minutes the Chapel was all but cleared, and the few people remaining sat quietly in their seats.

Security, followed closely by Schneider, came tearing through the side entrance.

"What happened?"

Johnson briefly detailed the events to Schneider and the security guards.

"Was an ambulance called?"

"Of course, but the man is dead. He must have died instantly."

Schneider shuddered slightly as he looked up at Goldstein's unnatural position on the lectern. "I'll have to get the homicide team down to take pictures and statements."

"We can't leave the body here too long, it has already caused some problems with the patients."

"It won't take long." Schneider spotted the phone in the corner and headed for it. Johnson looked at the back of the auditorium where Lowell had been seated . . . he was gone. As if in answer to the glance, Schneider posed the question as he got off the phone.

"Where's Lowell?"

"He was seated in the back before the conference began, but I don't know where he is now. He may have gone back to the ward with the patients. I told all the staff present to return as soon as the patients were settled."

"If he isn't back in ten minutes, my men are going to have to go and look for him."

Johnson made no comment. Staff began to file in one at a time. Johnson became more and more apprehensive as each staff member returned and John did not appear. Finally, just inside the ten-minute deadline, John arrived. He walked in the front of the auditorium where Schneider's men were already going over the area systematically. Schneider ignored him for the moment and addressed the staff. "There are two uniformed policemen at each exit. Please give your statement to them as you go out. We may have to contact you again at a later time. The staff began queuing up at the various exits.

Schneider spoke to Johnson. "How do you know they are all back?"

"You can check your statements against the sign-up sheet in the foyer of the Chapel."

John spoke for the first time. "There's only one problem with that."

Schneider responded, "And that is?"

"If the murderer was planning on killing Goldstein, he might not have signed the register."

"That's right," Johnson agreed.

"On the other hand, he would be taking a chance that someone might remember he was here, and it would be very suspicious if he did not sign up."

"I'm not sure we have to look that far," said Schneider, looking ominously at John.

John was in control of himself and didn't rise to Schneider's barb. "I was seated in the back of the Chapel. I would have to be a cat to get up in the front, kill Goldstein and return to my seat in total darkness in that short space of time."

"How long were the lights out, Doctor?" Schneider turned to Johnson.

"I don't know exactly, but it wasn't more than three minutes."

"Does anyone know why they went off?"

One of the security guards cleared his throat. The three men turned to the new source. "I don't know who turned them off, but I turned them back on."

"They were turned off?"

"Yes, at the fuse box in the basement. The main circuit breaker had been thrown."

"And that couldn't have been from an overload?"

"The only way you could overload the whole system would be if lightning hits the line between the building and the transformer."

Schneider was puzzled. "It had to be a two-man job then. No one could throw the circuit breaker, come up here in the dark, kill Goldstein and get away before the lights came back on."

"It seems highly unlikely," admitted Johnson.

"Plus, they would have to pass me," the guard interjected. "I started down as soon as the lights went out, and that's a narrow passage all the way back to the fuse box. As far as I know, that's the only way back here."

Schneider followed the security guard to the stairwell in the foyer and then down into the basement . . . the passageway was dark and narrow. No one could have passed the guard without brushing against him. The room at the end of the tunnel was also small and bare except for the three doors in the middle of each of the walls.

Schneider turned to the guard. "Where do these doors lead?"

"Everywhere."

"What do you mean?" questioned Schneider.

"They go into the tunnel system."

"What tunnel system?"

"The hospital tunnel system. Every building is connected by underground tunnels."

"Why is that?"

"Originally, as a security measure so that patients could not escape. Now some of them are used in bad weather to keep the patients out of the rain, but most of them are hardly ever used."

Schneider had an idea, but he pushed it to the back of his mind and turned his attention to the fuse box. There was nothing unusual about it except for some scratches on the main switch. "Is someone in Maintenance familiar with all of the electrical systems?"

"Tony, the foreman of the electrical shop. He also makes regular inspections of all the boxes. The date should be on the side of the box."

Schneider checked the list. The box had been inspected the previous month, and the initials TS were behind the date. "Are these his initials?"

"Yes."

"Would you have him come down here?"

"Okay."

"Before you go, are these tunnel doors locked?"

"They are supposed to be." The guard checked the doors. All of the doors were locked.

Schneider looked at the locks carefully. They were all rusted, and no fresh scratches could be seen around the key holes. "Do you have a key for these?"

"Yes."

"Would you open them please?" asked Schneider. The guard hesitated. "You can lock them again when you bring Tony back."

"Okay." The guard unlocked the doors and went in search of the electrician.

Schneider stood in front of the middle door. An unreasonable fear gripped him. He reached for the latch and then withdrew his hand again. This is ridiculous, he thought, but still hesitated. Finally, looking around sheepishly he pulled out his gun and opened the door. There was nothing on the other side but a narrow tunnel which vanished in the murky distance. He quickly surveyed the other two . . . the same. He looked carefully at the floors and saw no disturbance of the dust in the center or right, but the left-hand tunnel looked as though it had recently been swept. He shut the doors again. A careful inspection of the room produced nothing else. Shortly, he heard the guard and Tony coming down from the Chapel. The guard introduced Tony to Schneider and then returned upstairs.

"When was the last time you were down here?"

"It should be on the box," answered Tony.

"Yes, last month, but was that the last time?"

"Yes, I wouldn't come down here except on regular inspections or if there was a problem."

"And there hasn't been any problem?"

"No."

"Does everything look okay to you now? Be careful just to touch the edges."

Tony looked at the box on the outside and then checked the inside carefully. "Someone's been at it."

"How do you know?"

"The scratcheson the main breaker weren't there before."

"Are you sure?"

"Almost positive. That plastic is very tough, and it would take contact with a metal tool or something very hard to make them. I would have noticed. Also, there are scratches around two of the leads inside, and they are both a little loose." He pointed to two screws at the bottom of the circuit box.

Schneider looked carefully at the box again and then at the floor under the box. "Do you know what caused that?"

"It looks like the dust that comes down when you take a box off the wall."

"Why would anyone do that?"

Tony shrugged.

"Would you remove it, please?"

Tony shrugged again. "Okay." It only took a few seconds to unfasten the four screws holding the box to the wall. There was enough play in the main wire coiled into the wall to slide the box to the floor. Tony shined his light into the hole behind the box between the studs on either side. "There's something down there."

"What is it?"

"Looks like a wire with a loop on it."

"Can you get it out?"

"Easy." Tony took a coat hanger-like device out of his tool box and guided the hooked end through the loop in the wire. He pulled and the wire tightened. "It's heavy."

"Don't break it."

"I won't." Tony pulled steadily, and the loop came up to the hold so that he could grab it with his pliers. He pulled the wire out through the hole until a lead counterweight emerged. Attached to the counterweight was a clock with two wires coming from the back. Tony behaved like a kid with a new toy. "What the hell?"

"What is it?"

"A timing device to trip an electrical circuit."

"What circuit?"

Tony shined his flashlight into the hole again. "Here it is." He pointed to the solenoid at the back of the studded wall, then felt down the front and pulled up a piece of wood which was hinged down out of sight. "I've got it," said Tony gleefully.

"What?"

"Somebody hooked a wire up over the wall to the main circuit breaker, attached the timing device to the solenoid catch and powered it off the box itself. When the timer triggered the solenoid, the trapdoor dropped the weight, pulled the switch to the off position and the wire slipped off. The weight also pulled the clips off the screws in the box, and the whole device went down to the bottom of the wall."

"Very clever."

"Damn clever."

"I'll send the fingerprint crew down. Then you can replace the box." Schneider went back upstairs to notify the fingerprint crew and walked in on a confrontation between Johnson and the late Senator's entourage.

"But damn it, you should have told us about the threatening memo." The Senator's secretary was recovering from the initial shock and beginning to evaluate his position in all of this.

Dr. Johnson was getting a little ragged around the edges, dealing with all of the aspects of the situation. "We didn't know and, as a matter of fact, still don't know for sure that the memo was directed toward the Senator."

Schneider interjected, "The first memo and death might have been a coincidence but this seems to be a pretty clear-cut connection."

John had had very little to say up to this point but had been turning the events over in his mind and had come to some conclusions. "The note and Goldstein have a very clear relationship."

"Which is?" Schneider turned to John.

"The allusion to Moses is very appropriate. Goldstein's big push over the last several years has been to get mental patients out of the State hospitals. 'Let my people go.'"

"The people downtown are going to want answers to some very tough questions," continued the Secretary.

"Well, then you'd better run along and find out what they are and get back to us so we can answer them," said Johnson sarcastically, turning his back on the odious little man.

Schneider watched the Secretary retreat down the aisle. "I want you two to see something." He escorted John and the Superintendent down to the power room where the fingerprint crew was still dusting the box and doors for fingerprints. He explained the device to them. "That blows our two-person theory. At least it wasn't necessary for more than one person to be involved."

John's mind was racing again. He turned to Schneider. "What do you think the purpose of this device was?"

Schneider regarded him disdainfully. "That's obvious."

"Is it?" questioned John.

"To get the lights off so he could kill Goldstein."

"Of course, but why did he do it this way?"

"To throw us off the track, make us think there was more than one person involved."

"No."

"No?"

"No. A person clever enough to rig up this device would also be clever enough to avoid the mistakes which led you to finding it. The scratches on the switch could have been avoided by using an insulated wire for the tripping device. A battery-generated clock and solenoid would have avoided connections to the box and been a simpler installation. Also, he would have cleaned up the plaster dust when he replaced the fuse box."

"Then why did he do it this way?"

"Precisely to arrange things so that we would come to the exact conclusion which we have reached."

"Which is?"

"That we are dealing with a very clever fellow."

"Your paranoid personality again?"

"He's not my paranoid, but he is a paranoid and not a garden variety paranoid schizophrenic either."

"That's still just a theory," said Schneider. "And you seem to know a great deal about how Malleus thinks."

"You really are a Johnny-one-note, Schneider."

Johnson stepped in. "Would you two knock it off? We have some serious problems here and not just with this case. Schneider, if you're through with us we've got work to do."

"I'm not finished with you by a long shot, especially you, Doctor," looking at John, "but I have plenty to do myself. I'll get back to you later."

Johnson and Lowell left Schneider and went back to the Administration Building. John sat on the psychiatric couch in the corner of Johnson's office while the Superintendent paced up and down the room.

"John, you've got to find this guy. All hell is going to break loose down here in about ten minutes." He stopped. "It isn't you, is it?"

"Oh, hell."

"Okay, I'm sorry. But I'd be willing to bet that phone is going to ring and it's going to be the Governor. This hospital is hanging on by its fingernails as it is."

"They have been threatening to close us down for years."

"They still are, and the legislators who are pushing for it will have a field day with the murder."

"What do you want me to do?"

"Find Malleus."

"I know, but I can't do it looking through the records."

"You're sure?"

"Yes, even if Malleus is a patient, which is not all that certain, he is too clever to give himself away."

"Then you're giving up."

"No, I can't afford to. Schneider is really convinced it's me."

"What are you going to do?"

"I can't tell you. You wouldn't believe me anyway."

"For Christ's sake, John . . ."

"You're just going to have to let me handle it in my own way."

"I don't have much choice, do I?"

"None at all."

"Okay, but keep me informed of anything you come up with."

"Of course."

As John got up to leave, Peggy's voice came over the intercom. "Doctor, the Governor is on the line."

As John closed the door, he heard Johnson's weary voice, "Yes, Governor."

III

Schneider gave some final instructions to the police team in the chapel and then walked over to the Geriatrics Building. He rang the bell, and seconds later Judy let him in. "Good morning."

"Good morning, Mr. Schneider."

"Is Azahdi's secretary working today?"

"She's here, but there's not much work for her to do with Dr. Azahdi's death and John being gone most of the time." Judy looked a little vexed. This cop and robbers business was all well and good, but no one was minding the store and the operation was beginning to suffer.

"I'd like to speak to her again."

"She's in her office."

Schneider went past the nurses' station and looked into the receptionist's office. Debbie sat reading the latest Harlequin romance and didn't even look guilty as she closed the book. "What can I do for you, Mr. Schneider?"

"I would like to go over some points about the morning Dr. Azahdi died." Schneider noted the increased tension in Judy's posture and the hint of fear in her eyes.

"I've been over that several times with you and the other policemen."

"I know, but there are several things you seemed to be a little vague on."

"Such as?"

"What happened between the time Dr. Lowell left Azahdi's office and your discovery of his body."

"Nothing happened."

"What do you mean nothing? What exactly did you do?"

"What I usually do."

"Look, let's stop playing games. Did you or did you not leave the desk from the time Dr. Lowell came out of Azahdi's office until the time you went in with the mail and discovered his body?"

Judy stiffened and hesitated under Schneider's hawk-like glare. "Oh, all right. No, I didn't leave the desk."

"Did Dr. Lowell tell you to lie about it?"

"Absolutely not! As a matter of fact, when I told him I had led you to believe that I had left the office, he told me not to lie to you."

"He told you to tell me the truth?"

"Yes."

"Would you unlock Azahdi's office for me?"

Judy got up and opened the inner office.

Schneider looked carefully around the office again and then began going over the floor inch by inch, pulling the throw rugs back from the hardwood floors. Finally, he opened the closet door and examined the floor in the small enclosure. He seemed disappointed and returned to the outer office. "How do you get down into the tunnel system from this building?"

Debbie shrugged. "I don't know; I've never used it. It's down in the basement somewhere. Judy would know."

Schneider returned to the nurses' station. "Would you show me where the tunnel system is in the basement?"

"Sure." Judy led Schneider down the service stairway to the basement under the entrance of the mammoth Geriatrics Building. At the front of the service basement were the familiar three doors.

"Where do they lead?"

"The middle door opens into the main tunnel which goes all the way to the Administration Building. The door on the right goes over to the Long Term Care Center and the one on the left to the Nursing Unit."

"There is nothing toward the back?"

"Only the power room."

"May I see it?"

"I don't know if I have a key for that door."

"Would you check?"

Judy tried several keys without success and then tried the nursing key. The nursing key was second only to the master key in the number of different locks it would open. The maintenance door opened as she turned it in the lock. The room was crowded with boilers and electrical boxes. Schneider tried to judge how far back the room went under the building. It couldn't extend any further than Azahdi's outer office, if that far. In the back were several lockers which had been taken out of service and apparently stored here and used by maintenance men. Schneider looked at the floor around the lockers and noted some scratches on the floor which had not filled up with the dust which lay everywhere else in the room. He pulled the lockers away from the wall and behind them was another steel door. "Do you have a key for this door?"

"I don't know; I never knew there was another door back here," said Judy, frowning.

"It looks like one of the original locks; the skeleton key might fit it." The ancient door swung easily without a sound. Schneider looked at the hinges; they had been recently oiled, as had the lock. An unlighted tunnel extended twenty feet back to a ladder. "Hold this door open, please." Schneider went forward into the gloom. The ladder was a wrought iron antique going up against what seemed to be a solid ceiling. As Schneider ascended the ladder and pushed against the ceiling, however, it opened easily, and he found himself inside a closet. He recognized it immediately as the closet behind Azahdi's desk. Schneider whistled. He closed the trapdoor and rejoined Judy in the boiler room.

IV

John was worried about Randy. He had been one of the patients at the conference. As the hysterical aftermath of Goldstein's murder swept through the crowd, Randy had been one of the first to get caught up in it. Even though he was not one of John's charges, he had escorted him back to the Long Term Care Center. No one challenged his right to do so, because Randy, on one of his binges, was uncontrollable. John was fully aware that there was nothing he could do if Randy became really agitated, but Randy wasn't agitated; he was moaning and crying. There had been no anger or violence in his behavior.

John was anxious to get Randy back to the familiar ward and routine to see if there would be any lasting effects of the morning's violence. When John was able to return to the Long Term Care Center, Randy was in his room lying in the bed staring at the ceiling. "Let's go, Randy."

"I don't feel like it."

"You can't skip a workout – the meet's next week."

"I don't want to go to the meet."

"Why not?"

"They'll all make fun of me."

"I doubt it. You have a chance to win the Eastern championship. No one will make fun of that."

Randy turned to the wall. It sounded like he was crying softly. His huge shoulders shook the bed.

"What's bothering you, Randy – the business at the Chapel this morning?"

"No."

"Then what? You have been working hard for six months for this meet."

"I'm no good."

John was crestfallen. He saw the gains he had been making over the last year slipping away. "You're better than I am Randy, and I have been lifting for thirty years."

"I don't mean that."

"What do you mean?"

"I mean I'm no good. I'm bad."

"Bad?"

"I do bad things."

"What bad things, Randy?"

"I'm not allowed to tell. The Devil tells me to do them."

John was starting to get really worried. Randy had always vacillated between mania and depression, but hallucinations had never been part of his syndrome.

"You hear a voice telling you to do bad things?"

"The Devil."

"How do you know it is the Devil? Does he say he is the Devil?"

"He says he is the Devil, and he looks like the Devil."

"You see him too?"

"Of course I see him. I'm not crazy."

John thought this was debatable but let it pass. "When do you see him?"

"I'm not allowed to tell."

"Who told you that?"

"She . . ." Randy trailed off in confusion.

"Randy?"

"I'm not going to talk anymore."

"And the workout?"

"I don't feel like it."

"Okay, I'll check with you tomorrow." John left.

Down the hall the charge nurse saw him leaving Randy's room and picked up the telephone.

V

Queenie paced up and down her office waiting for Randy to arrive. Randy came sheepishly into the room. "Well?" Randy shuffled his feet and looked at the floor. "What did you and Dr. Lowell talk about?"

"Nothing."

"Come on, Randy."

"He wanted me to work out and I didn't want to."

"Is that all?"

"Uh-huh."

"You're lying to me Randy . . . Why?"

"I'm not lying." Randy continued to look at his feet."

"Don't make me angry, Randy. You know what I will do."

"Yes, ma'am."

"You didn't say anything to Lowell?"

"No."

"Okay. Next time I don't want to have to call you when you talk to him. You come down and tell me on your own."

"Yes, ma'am." Randy shuffled out of the office.

Queenie picked up the phone and punched out Fortunado's number. "Dick?"

"Yes?"

"Randy was just in here."

"Well?"

"He was talking to Lowell."

"What did he find out?"

"I don't think *he* found out anything, but he may have let something slip."

"Great! I thought you said you had him under control."

"I do, but he's so simple I don't think he can get anything out of Lowell."

"What did he tell him?"

"I don't know that Randy told him anything, but I have a feeling . . ."

"We may have to do something about Lowell."

"What?"

"I don't know yet . . . let's see what he does next."

Queenie hung up the phone and gazed out the window for a long time.

VI

Randy's refusal to lift threw John off stride. He went back to his office and called home. "Illanna?"

"Yes?"

"You going to be home for a while?"

"Sure."

"I'm coming home for lunch then."

"Aren't you working out?"

"Randy doesn't want to. Something happened this morning . . ."

"I know, I heard it on the radio."

"I'll be home in about ten minutes."

As John drove home he mused over Illanna's calm acceptance of Goldstein's murder.

She was busy at the sink when he walked in. She was wearing an apron and nothing else. John was used to the hospital gowns that tied down the back and the "Fanny flashers," but somehow this was more attractive than the usual Geriatrics show. He walked up and patted her affectionately.

"Uh-uh, lunch first."

John sighed. "We're getting like an old married couple."

"Speak for yourself, Gramps, but the eggs will get cold."

The omelet was good, but John had a hard time concentrating on it with Illanna sitting across from him wriggling around under the skimpy print apron. "This omelet is good, and the service is terrific."

"Oh, there's more." Illanna led John upstairs.

"I think I like dessert even better than the main course."

"You are a dirty old man."

John and Illanna made love playfully, forgetting completely the tightening web of horror at the hospital. Later John asked her why she had not been more upset about Goldstein's murder.

"Two reasons. First, I have been expecting something to happen, and I was relieved when it didn't seem to affect you directly. Second, in a strange sort of way, it seems right that Goldstein was murdered. That sounds awful, doesn't it?"

"It does sound rather odd. What do you mean it seems right?"

"Well, you remember how upset I got when Azahdi was killed? I hated that man, but I guess I was upset because in some way I felt that I had contributed to his death. When I heard about Goldstein's death it almost seemed inevitable -- like I had been waiting for it. Another thing was that I had no premonition of something bad happening."

John dismissed the last statement. He had problems in dealing with Gypsy's premonitions anyway and was not going to be thrown by the fact that she *didn't* have one.

"I'm worried about Randy."

"Yes, you said he didn't want to work out today."

"That's not too important. He has to start easing off anyway before the meet, but he may not compete."

"You're kidding! After all the work you two have gone through and all the trouble you had getting them to let him compete!"

"He says he doesn't want to. He's gone back into his self-pity routine again, but I don't think that's what's really bothering him. We had a very strange conversation."

"Why? What did he say?"

"He talked about being bad and doing bad things that the Devil told him to do."

"That's common enough, isn't it?"

"Oh, that kind of talk is quite common among schizophrenics but not coming from a manic-depressive and particularly not from Randy. He has never even had a paranoid delusional system, let alone auditory and visual hallucinations. His problem centers around his self-image. I'd swear he was talking about some real people and events, but that doesn't make sense . . . the Devil!"

"Let's see what the cards say." Illanna bounced off the bed and went over to the dresser, where she picked up a deck of tarot cards. Watching her naked body, John found himself distracted again, but she was going into her Gypsy mode so he steered his thoughts back to the problem.

"What are you going to do?"

"I'm going to read the cards for Randy." Illanna started laying out the cards.

"What exactly do the cards say?"

"Randy is under the influence of two people. One is this Rachel and the other is someone who controls her, more or less, and so has influence over Randy through her."

"Who is this second person?"

"It's very confusing. Let me tell you about Rachel first."

"Okay."

"Rachel is a witch."

"Spelled with a 'b'."

"No John, I'm serious. She is a witch and a fairly powerful one. I'm almost certain hers was the power I felt before."

"She's a witch like you?"

Illanna's eyes flashed dangerously. "No, she's not like me."

"You said she was a witch."

"Yes, but she practices black magic, and she is not just a dabbler. It's her approach to witchcraft."

"And you practice white magic."

"The only time I ever fooled with black magic was the time with Azahdi, and I learned my lesson."

"Okay, what about the man?"

"He is much more difficult and, in a way, more frightening."

"Frightening?"

"In some ways he has more power than Rachel but in others he has no power at all . . . he is just a shadow."

"I don't understand."

"I don't understand either, John. It is scary because there is so much undirected evil involved. Rachel is into black magic, and she directs the power she has for her own ends. She's good but only in the technical sense. She knows what she's doing. This other one has access to unlimited evil power but doesn't know it."

"How does all this relate to Malleus?"

"I don't know."

"Could he be Malleus?"

"It's certainly possible."

"It looks like I had better find out who the man is."

"I may be able to help you if you can narrow it down and bring me something which belongs to each of the people you think it might be."

"So I'm looking for someone who has influence over Rachel?"

"Right."

VII

Schneider's talk with Azahdi's secretary and his discovery of the trap door in the office hadn't changed his mind about Lowell. He would have arrested Lowell if the other access to the office hadn't been there, but its presence didn't get Lowell off the hook. It would have been easy for Lowell to go down into the basement and come up through the trap door himself.

The two problems were motive in the case of Azahdi's death and motive and opportunity in the case of Goldstein. It still nagged at Schneider that Lowell went back into Azahdi's office. If he was innocent, it could have been to look for another access, the same as he had done. On the other hand, if he was guilty he could have been looking for something else . . . Schneider decided to have another talk with the Superintendent.

Johnson had gotten rid of all the reporters and had stopped taking calls from downtown. He almost welcomed Schneider's call that he was coming over. At least Schneider was doing something positive.

"Come in, Lieutenant."

Schneider eyed the Superintendent suspiciously at this return to civility but accepted the break in the tension that had been growing between him and Johnson and Lowell.

"Have you made any progress?"

"Yes and no."

"Well give me the good news first; I could use some."

"I have found out how the murderer probably got into Azahdi's office."

"How?"

"There is a trap door in the closet behind Azahdi's desk that leads from the basement of the Geriatrics Building."

"Really! Well actually it's not too surprising. The whole hospital is riddled with underground passageways. I doubt if anyone knows where they all are."

"I guessed there might be when I saw the passages under the chapel, but it still doesn't clear Lowell."

"Really Lieutenant, I can't believe that John is involved in this. I have known him for years, and, even if he was angry at Azahdi, what would be his motive for killing Goldstein?"

"Goldstein is another matter. It would have been difficult for Dr. Lowell to have gotten up to the front of the Chapel in pitch black darkness, killed him and gotten back to his seat in such a short space of time. But even Azahdi is a problem as to motive. Lowell does not impress me as an impulsive man. He has a temper, but with his size and strength, if he acted physically against everyone he got mad at, there would be a string of bodies behind him a mile long. Whoever killed Azahdi had been planning it for some time."

"How do you know that?"

"The lock and the hinges on the door leading to Azahdi's office had been oiled recently. I can't imagine anyone cool enough to take a can of oil with them as they went to kill someone. I don't think it's even possible to oil the hinges on the trap door from underneath. Which means that someone had to be in Azahdi's office before the murder."

"Well then, what is Lowell's motive if not anger?"

"I don't know; that's why I came to see you. Why didn't Lowell like Azahdi?"

"There are probably many reasons, some of which might be hard for you to understand."

"Try me."

"Well to begin with, John loves his patients."

"Is that unusual?"

"In a way it is, yes. Most doctors become hardened through necessity, especially if they are in an area where a high percentage of their patients die. Geriatrics is a specialty where you do not get too close to the patients, because they die with great regularity."

"And Lowell is not hardened."

"Dr. Lowell is an exceptional man along many dimensions. As you may have observed, he has an ability to absorb pain physically and emotionally and does not seem to need to build up defenses against it. We had a talk about it one time, and he claims it is from weightlifting."

"His weightlifting makes him love his patients?"

"No, his weightlifting gives him the capacity to withstand pain. He says that in order to achieve anything in weightlifting you have to break through a pain barrier. When that happens, it's almost like an out of the body experience. You can step back and analyze the pain like another sensation."

"But I still don't understand how that affects his relationship with his patients."

"If you are really close to someone you take a terrible risk, because if you lose that person you suffer tremendous emotional pain. We call that pain grief. We cannot avoid, or should not avoid, that risk with family, but imagine how vulnerable you are if you look at three hundred Geriatrics patients as if they were your grandparents. John can do that and survive."

"What about Azahdi?"

"Azahdi was at the other extreme. He didn't even need to build up defenses, because he never cared about the patients in Geriatrics. John knew that, and it made him furious."

"Why did you keep Azahdi on then?"

Johnson looked at Schneider with wonder at his innocence. "We are lucky to get one quarter of the licensed physicians we need. We take in foreign doctors and keep them until their English improves enough for them to pass their medical boards and then we lose them. Azahdi was not a total disaster as a physician, even if he was an unfeeling bastard. If he hated everyone in the place, patients and staff alike, I couldn't have afforded to fire him."

Schneider was still not satisfied with the explanation of the bad blood between Azahdi and Lowell. "Okay. I can see a personality clash between Azahdi and Lowell, but it doesn't explain Lowell's behavior after the murder."

"What do you mean?"

"Lowell went back into Azahdi's office. He was looking for something, something real and tangible."

"Maybe he was looking for another entrance, the same as you did."

"If he is innocent, that is a perfectly logical explanation. but if he is guilty then he already knew about the entrance and was looking for something else."

"What do you want from me?"

"Your permission to go through Azahdi's papers and see if anything turns up."

"A fishing expedition? Most of that stuff is confidential and you would have to go case by case and get permission."

"I know that. That is why I am asking for your permission."

Johnson's impulse was to say no, both because he liked John and also because of his natural protective instinct when it came to patient-related information. But in the back of his mind still nagged John's "not yet" when he had said Schneider had not found a motive. Reluctantly he agreed to let Schneider search through Azahdi's papers, with the proviso that he stay out of actual patient's records.

CHAPTER SIX -- WEASEL

I

Schneider walked out of Johnson's office armed with the superintendent's approval to go through Azahdi's papers. He never got back to Geriatrics.

It was another beautiful spring day. The crystal clear air of a "Canadian High" accentuated the color contrasts. The cherry blossoms were in full bloom, hanging heavy on the trees, forming a pink cathedral over the entire length of the causeway between the Administration building and Geriatrics. Schneider was pleased with himself and more relaxed than he had been since he stepped on campus. He had almost forgotten her . . .

"Hello, Sonny."

Schneider stopped dead. Sitting on a bench off the causeway a tiny woman in a faded hospital dress was staring at him intently.

"Who . . . who are you?" stammered Schneider.

"You know me, Sonny – I'm your mother."

"D . . . d . . . don't be ridiculous." Schneider started to turn away.

"Don't go away Sonny. Come and sit with me."

A detached observer might have likened Schneider's movement to a mime being pulled by an invisible rope. It looked as if every fiber of his being wanted to go in any direction but toward that bench, and yet toward it he went and sat down beside the woman. "Why do you say you're my mother? I don't know you."

Tears welled up in the woman's eyes and began streaming down her cheeks. "I thought you were my son, I lost him years ago."

"What's your name?" The question was dragged involuntarily from the detective.

"Abigail."

Schneider's face had been ashen since he first heard the woman's voice, now it turned white. "Abigail what?"

"Abigail, Abigail, Fairy Tale, Fairy Tale."

The policeman rocked back and forth. Except for his clothes, the roles had been reversed. He looked like a patient and she the visitor.

"What's the matter, Sonny?"

"Nothing."

"Nothing the matter, nothing the matter, mad as a hatter, mad as a hatter." The woman's sing-song cadence voiced Schneider's darkest fears.

"Have you been here long?"

"Only a week, I don't belong here. My son is coming to pick me up."

Schneider looked at her more closely. She had a placid face, thin almost to emaciation. She could have been of any age from forty to sixty. There were no wrinkles in her face but her snow white hair made her *look* old. Her eyes were bright and blue and didn't quite focus.

"You said you lost your son years ago," Schneider contradicted.

"Oh yes, that's right. Years ago, years ago, white as snow, white as snow."

"Do you like it here?"

"Here?"

"This place."

The woman looked around her vaguely. "You know they steal your babies from the nursery."

"Who does?"

"The keepers."

"Who are the keepers?"

"Finders keepers, losers weepers."

Schneider was under control to the point where he could talk to the woman. He became more agitated, however, each time she broke from lucidity into her rhyming responses.

At a considerable distance an interested observer watched the scene being played out. Lowell was in the nursing station at the back of the psychiatric treatment center. He wondered at Schneider's apparent interest in the patient. He pointed out the couple to the charge nurse. "Do you know who that patient is?"

"Oh, that's Abigail, Abigail," she chuckled.

"Abigail, Abigail?"

"That's what she calls herself. I don't know her last name. She is not from this Center."

"I wonder what Schneider finds so interesting in her conversation," John mused half to himself.

Abruptly Schneider left the woman and headed for his car.

II

Schneider drove home in a daze. He didn't check in with headquarters or leave any instructions for the team at the hospital. The worst had happened – he had seen his mother. When the call had first come in from the hospital and he had been assigned to Azahdi's case, he knew there was a possibility that he would see her. She had been in the hospital continuously since he was fourteen and in and out all the time he was growing up. His father's drinking had started with her first schizophrenic break, and his death on an alcoholic ward pretty nearly coincided with her last admission. Schneider was intellectually aware of the consequences a schizophrenic mother and an alcoholic father could have on the personality development of a child. He had Abnormal Psychology in college and read everything he could get his hands on about schizophrenia during his years on the police force. Emotionally, he was still going through the hell of that childhood. Although he prided himself on his coolness and logic, these defenses were a thin veneer over what Johnson would call a "basket of worms."

Once he got home he began to drink brutally, seeking the same refuge of insensibility his father had sought – his father who had come to him in drunken self-pity – come to a child who loved and longed for a mother who was alternately loving and accepting, then callously rejecting. No amount of intellectualizing could erase the hell spawned within that child. The only escape was the escape of his father and this time didn't come. The logic slipped away and unleashed the introverted fears and self-hatred – the fears of madness – the hatred for a child so unlovable even a mother rejected him. When the self-hatred became unbearable he turned it against the world and it came to rest on Lowell – Lowell with his smug logic – Lowell the keeper, "finders keepers" – Lowell the murderer. Schneider fumbled through the telephone directory and dialed John's number.

Illanna answered. "Hello."

"I want to talk to Lowell," Schneider slurred.

"*Dr.* Lowell is not at home. Who is this?"

"Schneider."

"Oh."

"Where ish he? Yeah, up there killing someone elsh."

"Schneider! What's wrong with you? You sound drunk."

"I am drunk, but not so drunk you can pull the wool over my eyes."

"What are you talking about?"

"You two are in it together. You two with your witchcraft and your malleus, malleus." Schneider began to sob and slammed down the receiver.

"Schneider? . . . Schneider?" Illanna hung up and dialed John's office.

"I'm sorry, Dr. Lowell is not in at the moment. May I take a message?"

"This is an emergency. Would you have him paged, please?" Illanna drummed her fingers nervously on the table as the minutes slipped by.

"I'm sorry, Dr. Lowell doesn't answer his page. May I take a message?"

"Yes, tell him to call home when he gets in."

III

Illanna grabbed the phone book and found Schneider's address. Without analyzing her actions, she jumped in her van and headed for his apartment. From the beginning Schneider's phone call had not awakened anger in Illanna. The words were meant to do that, but Schneider sounded so desperate. A crisis intervention worker would have recognized that desperation as a cry for help. So did Illanna, but not on a conscious level. She was almost to the apartment when she began to question what she was doing. She was driven by a compelling force, however, and she followed her instincts. Schneider lived on the second floor of a brownstone duplex which was right on the street. Illanna read the card in the foyer, ran up the steps and pounded on the door.

"Schneider?"

"What ish it?"

"Open the door."

"Jush a minute."

She heard a crash and stumbling around. The door opened a crack.

"Oh, ish you."

Illanna pushed into the room and Schneider almost fell over backwards.

"What duyu want?"

"Are you alright?"

"Jush fine."

Illanna began to feel embarrassed. Here she was in a drunk's apartment – a man she hardly knew – for what? She plowed ahead. "You didn't sound fine on the phone."

"Phone?"

"You called Dr. Lowell."

"Thas right – the Doc." Schneider was groping back through the haze, trying to remember. "I wanted to ashk about . . . ashk him about . . ."

"What?"

"My mother."

"Your mother?"

"Yeah."

"What about her?"

"If she will ever get out of that place."

"What place?"

"The hospital."

"Your mother is at the State Hospital?"

"Yeah."

Illanna sat down in an overstuffed chair and Schneider collapsed on the couch. Her thoughts were reeling from this entirely new twist. "How long has your mother been at the hospital?"

"Long time . . . twenty, twenty-five years."

"And you just found this out?"

"No, I knew where she was." Schneider was slowly becoming more lucid. As the rational processes took hold a profound depression began to set in.

"When was the last time you saw her?"

"I told you . . . years ago."

"You mean you never visited her in all that time?"

"That's right." Schneider's voice was defiant but his eyes were pleading – for what – understanding, forgiveness? Illanna couldn't tell. "I was only fourteen when she went the last time. My father wouldn't let me see her."

The *last* time. Illanna began to see the hell Schneider's childhood must have been. "So, you saw her today?"

"Yes."

"Did you go to see her or just meet her by accident?"

"I just met her."

"And she recognized you?"

"I don't know . . . she called me Sonny. That's what she used to call me."

"But you recognized her?"

"Oh yes. I'll never forget *her*."

Illanna looked at him hard. The emotion lying just under Schneider's usual icy façade was pushing hard. She wanted to go over to the couch and hold this pain-racked man – this child who had never *been* a child and so could never be a man. She rejected the ridiculous notion which would probably have been misinterpreted in any event. "Are you alright, Schneider?"

"Sure . . . no . . ." Schneider snarled off in confusion. Why should he spill his guts to this . . . witch? But the condescension wouldn't wash. He was desperate to talk to someone and for some reason she seemed concerned. She should hate him but she didn't. Normally his pride alone would have rejected help from such a quarter. The alcohol, however, had lowered some of his defenses and the pain inside was searching desperately for expression.

"Why did you want to talk to Dr. Lowell really?"

"I wanted to ask him . . . ask him if schizophrenia is inherited." There it was out:

the dark question that Schneider had kept festering in the Freudian recesses of his mind since he had learned the name of the madness.

"I don't think . . ." It was Illanna's turn to trail off in confusion. She knew as much and probably more than most laymen about mental illness and she was aware of some of the controversy surrounding the nature-nurture etiology of schizophrenia. The question was certainly unresolved. What was the best answer to give Schneider? John should be here talking to him, not her. She changed her tack and took up John's Rogerian approach. "What do you think?"

"I have read a lot about it," said Schneider.

Illanna noticed for the first time the floor to ceiling book shelves behind the couch. The titles were not what one might expect to find in a policeman's home. It looked more like John's library.

"No one will come out definitely one way or the other."

"Do you think you are in danger . . ." Illanna didn't know how to phrase the question.

"Of losing my mind?"

"Yes."

"Not usually . . . but today . . ."

"When you saw your mother?"

"I don't know what's happening to me. Ever since I have been going to the hospital I don't seem able to control . . ."

"But that's only natural – your concern for your mother, your guilt . . ."

"Guilt! . . . for what? She left me . . . all I ever wanted was . . ." Schneider began to cry. Illanna couldn't stand it. She went over to the couch and put her arms around him and rocked him like a baby. Schneider sobbed on her shoulder for a couple of minutes and then got up and stood looking out of the window. Illanna felt his embarrassment. He was still shaking but desperately trying to bring himself under control. Gradually he succeeded.

"Schneider? Are you all right?"

"Yes, thank you." An icy formality had crept into his voice.

"Can I do anything for you?"

"No, I'm fine now."

"Are you sure?"

"Yes, I'm sorry to put you to so much trouble."

Illanna felt the wall between them, stronger than it had been when they were strangers. She rose to leave.

"Do you want me to have John call you?"

"No. That was all nonsense. I shouldn't drink."

"Well . . . I'll see you."

"Sure."

Illanna left him staring out of the window at the gray street.

IV

When Illanna pulled into the driveway, John's car was already there. He met her at the door. His brow was furrowed with concern. "What's the matter? Where have you been?"

"At Schneider's."

"Schneider's!"

"Yes, he called about an hour ago. I tried to call you at the hospital."

"I got the message. They said it was an emergency. What emergency?"

"Schneider called and accused you and me of murder."

"We knew that was his opinion. What was the emergency?"

"John . . . I don't think that's why he called at all."

"What, then?"

"Did you know Schneider's mother is at the hospital?"

"What do you mean?"

"She's a patient at the hospital. Has been for most of Schneider's life."

"So that's it."

"What?"

"It explains why Schneider has been so uptight since this business started. I knew there was something. That must have been his mother he was talking to this afternoon."

"You saw him talking to her?"

"Yes, I was in the Psychiatric Treatment Center checking Andy's admission record and I saw Schneider from the window. He talked to a woman for a few minutes and then took off like a shot."

"What did the woman look like?"

"I was too far away, but she had white hair so she was certainly old enough to be his mother." John whistled. This whole business was getting more and more complicated. John brought himself back to Illanna. "Did he tell you this on the phone?"

"No, he just accused us of the murders."

"Then why on earth did you go over to his place?"

"He sounded drunk on the phone. He admitted he was drunk, and he was so desperate."

"Desperate?"

"Yes, I don't know how else to describe it. He sounded as if he were on the brink of something awful."

John was puzzled. Why was this suddenly a crisis if Schneider's mother had been there so long?

"Tell me exactly what he said, what he did and how he looked."

Illanna squirmed a little. She didn't know how John would react to the hugging episode, but she related everything from the phone call to her exit from Schneider's apartment. John interrupted her several times to ask if she could tell how Schneider was feeling at a given instant. He glossed right over Illanna's motherliness, which she would have resented if John hadn't been so intent on the details of the episode. "Why is all this so important, John? Does it have something to do with Malleus?"

"No . . . I don't think so, but unless Schneider is a different breed of cat than the ones I have been treating for the last fifteen years, he is in serious trouble."

"What kind of trouble?"

"Emotional. Schneider impressed me from the beginning as an extremely controlled person."

"Look who's talking."

John brushed the interjection aside. "If what we are learning about him is accurate, he should be a classic case of the child raised by a schizophrenic mother. She would be alternatively over-protective and loving, then punishing and rejecting. Unless the father was a stabilizing influence, the emotional scars would go very deep. The fact that Schneider was unable to come up and see his mother for all these years means that he has never dealt with his feeling about her or himself. Add to that his fear that he might suffer from the same illness and you have someone who as you put it is on the brink. The question is the brink of what?"

"He seemed all right when I left."

"That's what scares me the most. He was shaken by meeting his mother. His usual defenses weren't sufficient to deal with the confrontation, so he got drunk. When he was drunk he was vulnerable, and he let the wall down completely. For a couple of minutes he was a child again."

"And . . . and I was his mother," gasped Illanna.

"Exactly. I don't know if Schneider can live with admitting that much weakness."

"You don't mean . . ."

"Yes, I'm afraid he is a very good candidate for suicide."

"Oh no! John, it's my fault."

"No. If you hadn't gone over there, who knows what would have happened. He might have drunk himself to death. He may be back on an even keel, but I'm still worried."

"Why? As I said, he seemed perfectly alright when I left."

"What kind of alright? Happy? Relaxed? . . . What?"

"No . . . more resigned . . . fatalistic . . . oh!"

"Exactly. If you had been on the end of as many suicide phone calls as I have, you'd know what that resignation was, the true meaning of fatalism."

"What can we do?"

"I don't know if there is anything we can do. We don't have any indication that he is actually going to commit suicide. I may be over-dramatizing the whole thing."

The phone rang stridently, breaking into John's quandary.

"Hello." John covered the mouthpiece. "It's Johnson."

"Yes? . . . No, I haven't seen him, but he did call here earlier. Isn't he home? . . . I see. I'll tell him if he calls again."

John hung up the phone, grabbed Illanna's hand and dragged her to the car.

"Where are we going?"

"Schneider's."

V

Illanna directed while John explained the phone call. "Schneider didn't report back to the station, and he didn't tell his men he was leaving the hospital. When they called his apartment he didn't answer."

"Then he may have . . ."

"He may have done it."

John wheeled the Jaguar expertly through the traffic. Fortunately no traffic cops clocked him through town. It had taken Illanna twenty minutes to get to Schneider's. John made it in ten. They ran up the old stairs two at a time and knocked on the door. No answer.

"He's in there."

"How do you know?"

"He's in there!" John took a half step back across the hall and threw his two hundred and twenty-five pounds against the door. The catch splintered the frame, and the door sagged open. Schneider lay sprawled on the couch. A half empty bottle of Jack Daniels was on the table next to an empty prescription bottle. John read the label. "Sleeping pills. Call Johnson."

"Shouldn't I call the hospital?"

John checked Schneider's breathing and made a decision. "Not yet. Get Johnson."

"What should I tell him?"

"Tell him to get over here and bring his little black bag on the double."

Schneider was breathing regularly and his pulse was strong. John slapped him across the face several times. Schneider moaned and opened his eyes. "Come on, Schneider, get up."

"What are you doing here?"

"Just dropped by to wake you up. Where's the kitchen?"

Schneider nodded toward the café doors at the rear of the apartment. John dragged him across the room. He found some mustard in the refrigerator and soon had Schneider emptying his stomach in the bathroom. Illanna got through to Johnson, and ten minutes later he arrived.

"What's going on?"

Hurriedly John explained the situation.

"Why didn't you call an ambulance?"

"He didn't seem too far under."

"You shouldn't be making those kinds of judgments."

"I know," said John. "But from what you said Schneider is AWOL and already in trouble downtown. If they knew he tried to commit suicide, it might be the end of his career. Schneider without a job might as well be dead."

"Okay . . . what did he take and how much?"

"I don't know how many he took, but he threw up quite a few and they weren't dissolved yet so he must have taken them and passed out drunk."

Johnson seemed satisfied. He gave him a shot of caffeine and prepared to leave. "You know the routine. Keep him walking, give him some coffee and don't let him sleep for a couple of hours."

"Right."

As Johnson was heading for the door he looked at Illanna for the first time. John hadn't offered to introduce her and she had stayed pretty much out of the way.

"Don't I know you?" he queried.

"I don't believe we've met. I'm Illanna Romanowsky."

Somewhere in the back of his mind a switch clicked but Johnson couldn't recall where that name and face had come together. "Give me a call at home tonight, John, when Schneider straightens out."

It was an hour of walking and pouring coffee down the detective before the booze wore off enough to talk to Schneider.

"Now . . . what is all this nonsense?" chided John.

"I imagine she's told you everything," Schneider said nodding toward Illanna.

"She told me about your mother," John assented, "but what about the pills?" John took on the disapproving parent role. He hadn't worked out his strategy in his own mind for dealing with the situation, but this mild disapproval felt right so he went with it.

Schneider was on the defensive. "Sometimes I need sleeping pills to get to sleep."

"A whole bottle?"

"There weren't that many in it."

"Quit fencing, Schneider . . . you were looking for an easy way out. Let's find what you want out of. Illanna said you wanted to talk to me, so talk."

"I just wanted to know if schizophrenia was inherited."

"That's not an easy question to answer, but I can answer the question you really want to ask."

"Which is?"

"Whether you are going to become a schizophrenic."

There was a significant pause as Schneider waited for John to continue. He didn't. Finally Schneider broke down. "Well, am I?"

"No."

"How can you be so sure?"

"Look, you've read a few books and articles on schizophrenia. I've read them all. I have been around all types of mental illness for half of my life. I have yet to meet someone who had his first schizophrenic break at your age. With your background, you would be a prime candidate for schizophrenia and not just genetically. You haven't had a break and you won't."

Schneider looked as if a weight had been removed from his shoulders.

"That doesn't mean that you are out of the woods, though."

"What do you mean?"

"Attempted suicide is not the hallmark of mental health."

"I wasn't trying to commit . . ." he looked John in the eye. "Oh, all right. Maybe I wasn't all that anxious to wake up again."

"Okay, that's out in the open. Now why didn't you want to wake up?"

"You know . . . I was afraid I was losing my mind."

"No, Schneider. That's not it."

"What then?"

"How did you feel when you were talking to your mother?"

"Oh God!" Schneider buried his face in his hands.

"That's what you were trying to escape, and that's what you have to learn to live with."

"How?"

"By understanding it."

"How do I go about that?"

"You didn't come to me for help. Under the present circumstances we are not likely, nor do I think it advisable, that we get into a therapeutic relationship. What I can do is lay out the situation as I see it, and you can do what you want about it."

"Okay."

"Keep in mind that even if my interpretation of the situation is correct and you accept it, it will not change the way you feel. It may change the way you *think* about the way you feel and in the long run may help."

"I understand."

"In order for a child to face the world with confidence, he or she has to have a stable relationship with it. The best relationship is a nurturing one. That is, the world provides the child with what it needs when it needs it in a fairly predictable fashion. The child learns to trust. Once this trust is established, the child can learn to tolerate disappointments and exceptions because the fundamental faith is there.

"The next best situation is a fairly predictable hostile environment. The child can also learn to adjust to this. It is unlikely that the child will be happy nor is it likely the child will ever be satisfied and happy as an adult. But he can learn to cope and even be successful because of the consistence. He knows if he behaves in certain ways there will be a predictable result.

"Now we come to the child of the mother who has schizophrenia. Generally such a mother is alternately nurturing and rejecting of the child. The alternation is not based on the child's behavior. It is based on the illness. The fluctuations of the illness are not tied to reality or a logical process. The child needs to be loved and accepted and sometimes he is, but he is also rejected. He is faced with an insolvable problem, what psychologists call an approval-avoidance conflict. The problem is how to behave in order to be loved. Since there is no consistent response to whatever he does, the child eventually concludes that he is unlovable. This process is insidious for several reasons. If it begins when the child is very young and non-verbal he can only experience the alternate nurturance and rejection emotionally. Later, when he can verbalize it, it is too late to reason his way out of the problem because the emotions are tied to objects and situations without words to describe them or verbal memories of them.

"Another insidious aspect of the process is the nature of the approach-avoidance conflict itself. The mother is both the object of reinforcement (love) and punishment (rejection). The child cannot escape from the situation because reinforcement and punishment reside in the same object. To escape the punishment he also has to leave the source of love. He becomes an emotional yo-yo.

"Finally, no child is in a position to structure his environment to suit himself. He is dependent upon grown-ups (parents) to do that for him. If they have no control over themselves, it stands to reason they will have little or no control over what happens to the child.

"No one can live constantly with the feeling that they are unlovable. There are many ways of dealing with such feelings. From your library you are obviously aware of Freud's explanation for how we deal with unacceptable feelings. From his secondary list of defense mechanisms you seem to have chosen denial and isolation. They are powerful psychic tools, but they never work completely. You pay a terrible price in other areas. However, in the presence of the original cause of your feelings, the defenses broke down and didn't work at all."

"So what should I do?"

"Accept your mother for what she is, a woman with chronic schizophrenia who may never be any better than she is right now, but who loves you and is fighting to get hold of reality. Accept yourself as a victim of circumstance."

"I understand and can accept much of what you say, but will it change the way I feel?"

"It took many years to develop the coping mechanisms that have broken down. It will take years to develop better ones. I am not your therapist, and I don't think you want me to be, particularly under the present circumstances. I can recommend several very good people if you want to get into formal therapy."

"I don't know . . ." Schneider was struggling with the magnitude of the revelations he had heard from John. John had in fact appealed to Schneider's primary defense mechanism which was intellectualization. He could isolate the information about himself and turn it around, looking at it from all angles. John knew it would not make him feel better because of the deep-rooted and primitive nature of those feelings, but it gave Schneider a *rational* reason for feeling the way he did, and that was an excellent temporary crutch.

"I'm not recommending that you go into therapy," said John, but there *is* something that you had better do immediately. Get yourself squared away with your department."

"The Department!" Schneider was jerked back into reality.

"You apparently didn't call off and they have been looking for you."

"You didn't tell them . . . "

"We have told them nothing."

"But they will find out from Johnson's report."

"I don't think Johnson is going to make a report."

"But he has to . . ."

"Are you going to report him if he doesn't?"

The limb that Lowell and Johnson were out on suddenly became apparent to Schneider. By now they should have reported the apparent suicide. They could both lose their licenses. He was confused by their motivation. "Why did you two conceal the suicide attempt?"

"What would have happened to you if the department had found out you had tried to kill yourself?"

Schneider reflected on department policy. "I might have lost my job eventually. At the very least I would have been taken off active field duty."

"How would you have made out on inactive duty or no duty at all?" John queried.

"I don't know . . . "

"I do," said John. So did Schneider.

"After all I've tried to do to you, why should you help me?" Schneider was bewildered by the logical contradiction of Lowell's behavior.

"Don't make yourself out to be a special case. What's the sense in stopping you from committing suicide in such a way as to ensure your future suicide?"

"But I have been trying to prove that you are a murderer!"

"I know. That's your job. I can't sympathize with your aim in this instance. My job sometimes is to keep people from killing themselves. I don't have to *like* the people or approve of them any more than you have to *dislike* the people you have to deal with."

One consequence of Schneider's emotional isolation was that he didn't have any friends. It had never struck him as peculiar, since his job occupied all of his thoughts and most of his waking hours. A new emotion was forcing itself upon his already overburdened system. He had given Lowell a grudging respect from their first meeting. The respect grew out of his recognition of John's competence and dedication, which was Schneider's yardstick for everyone. Now he was beginning to *like* John. This was a new experience. Under the present circumstances it was not a wholly pleasant experience either.

"I don't dislike the people I deal with," said Schneider defensively.

"You don't like them very much either, though, do you?" John looked straight at Schneider. Schneider felt he was looking straight through him.

"I don't *have* to like anyone."

"Oh, but it would be nice to be able to, wouldn't it?" Schneider was feeling uncomfortable again. He had been through an emotional ringer and couldn't deal with this new concept. John saw the conflict and backed off.

"Anyway, this is all irrelevant. Are you okay now?"

"Yes."

"I don't have to check up on you?"

"No."

"If you start feeling upset again I would appreciate a call before you consider the booze and pill routine again. I really don't see you as a person who takes the easy way out."

"Don't worry, I won't do that again."

"Okay. One more thing. If you consider seeing your mother again I would like to talk to you about it first. In the meantime I will review her case so that I can give you some helpful information."

"I don't need any help."

"I didn't necessarily mean help for you."

"Oh!" Schneider looked down at the rug.

John and Gypsy left Schneider's when they were sure the alcohol and pills had worn off. Illanna had said very little during the entire episode at Schneider's. She had learned a great deal about John. Illanna had loved John

for a long time. At first she could not untangle
her feelings. She was grateful to him for
rescuing her from the hospital and had what
she considered a peculiar sexual attraction for
this bear of a man. She didn't respect him as
a professional. The lack of respect was her
defense against John's attack on *her* beliefs.
The trouble between them always grew out of
John's condescending attitude toward the
occult and her belief in it. John had become
more tolerant of those beliefs and recently had
begun to gradually accept them and even
come to her for help. Her tolerance for
"Psychology" had not kept pace. Now she
began to appreciate John's approach for the
first time.

As they drove home John looked over at her
and asked, "What are you grinning at?"

"You're not as dumb as you look."

"Thank God for that," laughed John. "To what
do I owe this unusual vote of confidence?"

"You helped Schneider very well. I wouldn't
have known what to do."

"I didn't do that much. Schneider is an
extraordinary man."

"Extraordinary in what way?"

"What we just saw was the breakdown in a
magnificent defense system. Not one person
in a thousand with Schneider's background

could function at all. Schneider not only functions but is a very competent person."

"But he has paid a price." Illanna had been paying attention. It was John's turn to grin appreciatively.

"Yes, a terrible price. He cannot deal with emotions so he blocks them out. I doubt if he has ever had a friend or loved a woman."

"Will he be alright now?" Illanna asked the question as one asks an expert. John felt the shift and the last barrier between them was gone.

"As long as he stays away from his mother. His system has worked for many years and should continue to work if it isn't strained past its limits. Apparently only his mother can do that."

"You know, it's funny," mused Illanna. "Schneider's right. We shouldn't be helping him."

"Like you don't help a drowning man because he's a tax collector," said John.

VI

Schneider slept. He slept the dreamless sleep of exhaustion, but not before he had called headquarters and explained his absence. His jumbled explanation of following up a lead was accepted because of his past work record. When he awoke, the early morning sun was first beginning to peek over the brick and wooden turrets of the Victorian row house across the street.   He was still on the couch. He made himself some coffee, showered and shaved and, except for a splitting headache, felt almost human. He began to plan his visit to the hospital. He had to go back, but the hospital didn't hold the terror for him that it had. He could now plan strategies for staying away from his mother until he felt he could deal with the situation. He would find out where she was, her schedule, haunts, and so forth from John. John? What happened to Lowell? Schneider chided himself for the softened feeling he had toward the psychologist.

A new reality began to dawn on the detective. He didn't *want* John to be guilty! As this revelation sank in, Schneider had new doubts. This kind of sentimentalism was foreign and abhorrent to him. Since when did he care who was guilty as long as he caught them? No matter how he turned it over in his mind he could not shake the feeling . . . feeling? More confusion.

This wouldn't do. Not professional. Must forge ahead with the investigation. Schneider screwed himself up to the task of going through Azahdi's papers. After all, there probably wouldn't be anything anyway. He drove around the back of the hospital, giving the administration complex a wide berth. Judy greeted him pleasantly and he smiled in return. Judy looked startled.

"What's the matter?" Schneider asked.

"I don't know . . . you look different."

"It's been a rough couple of days."

"No . . . you look fine. It's just . . . I never saw you smile before."

"I smile all the . . . actually you're right – I don't smile much." Schneider was startled by the truth of this statement. He was still smiling and his face *felt* different.

"So what's the good news?"

"Good news?"

"That made you smile?"

"I don't know . . . yes I do, you smiled at me."

"Don't people usually smile at you?"

"My business is usually pretty grim."

"I guess that's right. What about when you're not conducting business?"

"That's funny. I never thought much about it before, but I'm almost always conducting business."

"You must have a lousy union," Judy laughed. Schneider laughed too. He laughed and laughed. He laughed way out of proportion to the thin joke.

Judy's light banter turned to concern. "Are you alright?"

"Sure." Schneider brought himself under control. "I guess I don't laugh much either." He looked at Judy and saw something in her eyes that hadn't been there before. Schneider cleared his throat. "I have to look in Azahdi's office."

"Okay." Judy flipped over the counter exit and brushed against Schneider as she passed. An accident? Schneider's confusion returned.

"Do you suspect John?"

"I really shouldn't discuss the case." He was trying to sound stern but it came out apologetic.

"I know," said Judy, "but you know John really is incapable of hurting anyone."

"Normally I think you're right," admitted Schneider, "but beneath all the logic he is a passionate man. Under the proper circumstances that passion could turn to violence."

"What would the proper circumstances be?"

"If someone he cared about was threatened."

"But that's just it," said Judy. "John cares about everybody."

"Everybody? What about Azahdi?"

Judy paused. "You're right – he didn't care much for Azahdi. That was because Azahdi didn't care much for our residents."

"That's what I mean."

"I still don't think John could ever hurt anyone physically. Did he ever tell you about his marshmallow-ball bearing theory of personality?"

"No," laughed Schneider. "What the hell is that?"

"John says that everyone is made of layers. Some people are hard on the outside but soft underneath, the ball bearings with marshmallow centers. Some people are soft on the outside but hard underneath, the marshmallow-covered ball bearings. Some people are hard all the way through, the steel-jacketed ball bearings."

"Which is John?"

"John's a marshmallow covered marshmallow."

"I don't know – I've broken my teeth on him a couple of times already." Judy opened Azahdi's office and left Schneider to search through Azahdi's desk.

In strict adherence to Johnson's instructions, he avoided any papers which looked like they were patient-related. After rummaging through the desk for half an hour he had found nothing which was in any way related to John or the case. He was about to give up on the desk when he remembered the last place to look. He pulled the center drawer all the way out and set it on the floor.   Peering in the dark rectangle he saw a couple of crumpled sheets of paper at the back of the recess. He reached back, pulled them out and smoothed them on the blotter. They were both sheets from a memo pad, but the scribbled note on one of them jumped out at him. "Call Goldstein . . . Have the goods on Lowell." Schneider slumped back in the chair. There it was – not only the hint of a motive for Azahdi's murder but a connection to Goldstein as well. A sick feeling swept over him. He tried to step back from himself. This is what he wanted – a motive. Now he had motive and opportunity in Azahdi's death and motive in Goldstein's – maybe. Proof of opportunity in Goldstein's case, discovery of the motive of "the goods" and John was nailed. So if everything was going so good why was he feeling so bad?

He carefully put the note in a plastic baggie along with another hand written note signed by Azahdi. He put the desk back in order and closed up the office. He looked pretty grim as he approached the nursing station.

"You found something?" Judy's concern was evident.

"I'm afraid so. Is there somewhere we can talk?"

Judy led Schneider back to the nursing break room. "Well?"

"First let me level with you. I shouldn't be discussing this with anyone. If you let on I could be in serious trouble."

"I understand..."

"I wish I did. Two days ago I wouldn't have considered talking to anyone about this or any aspect of the case. A lot has happened in the last couple of days."

"You're starting to like John, aren't you?"

"I guess so. That shouldn't have anything to do with it though."

The look was back in Judy's eyes. "Why is it so hard for you to like anyone?"

"It's not . . . I don't know." Schneider put his face in his hands. Judy came over to him, raised his head and kissed him.

"Don't feel sorry for me."

"That's not what I feel for you." Schneider pulled her down gently to the couch and kissed her longingly. Judy broke it off.

"That's more like it, but we can't pursue it here." They both backed off and looked at each other in the new light of understanding.

"Now . . . what did you find?" Schneider pulled out the note.

Judy read it through the plastic. "Okay, but what does it mean?"

"It means, at least, that Azahdi had 'something on' John and was planning to tell Goldstein."

"But what's the connection between Goldstein and Azahdi?"

"I was hoping you would help with that," said Schneider. Judy thought for a minute. "I haven't any idea what the connection was, but there must have been one."

"How do you know that?"

"Well . . . there have been several messages left in the last few months for Azahdi to call Goldstein."

"You didn't tell me that before," Schneider was mildly reproachful.

"I didn't think of it before. You have no idea how many calls go through here. Hundreds a day."

"I could arrest John on the basis of this note."

"You don't know that it really represents a motive."

"True, but it's one more coincidence piled on top of many others, and it's the first connection between Goldstein and Azahdi."

"So. Are you going to arrest John?"

"Not yet. Three reasons. First, I don't know the nature of the motive or the connection between Goldstein and Azahdi. Second, I still can't see how John could have gotten to Goldstein to kill him."

"What's the third reason?"

"That's the one that doesn't make any sense."

"What is it?"

"I don't think he did it."

"Why doesn't that make sense?"

"Because so far he's the only suspect and everything points to him."

"So why don't you think he did it?"

"I don't know. I don't usually form opinions one way or the other."

"I know what your problem is, Bob."

"What?"

"You're turning into a *mensch.*"

Schneider was momentarily offended. Then he laughed. "A couple of days ago I would have been insulted. I always considered myself to *be* a human being. I guess I never really knew what that word meant before."

Judy stroked the hair back from his forehead. "What are you going to do now?"

"I have to keep looking. I honestly hope I find another angle to this case. If I don't, I am going to have to arrest John sooner or later. Sooner, with the heat the department is getting from the Governor over Goldstein. I can't sit on this note for very long and as soon as I turn it in the chief will order me to arrest him."

"What about us?"

"There is an 'us', isn't there?" There was wonder in Bob's voice.

"Yes. There is an 'us'."

"Can I see you tonight?"

"Any night."

Schneider made arrangements to pick her up for dinner after work. "Is John in now?"

"I think he's in his office."

Schneider went across the hall and knocked on John's door.

"Come in."

"Good morning." Schneider's manner was outwardly formal but John noticed the masklike hardness was gone from his face. A myriad of emotions played around his mouth and eyes.

"How are you feeling today?"

"I have a headache."

"I bet. The world looks a little better to you today?"

"*Sure* of it."

"Oh?"

Schneider paused, trying to find the right way to get into the note. "I was looking through Azahdi's desk."

John didn't respond.

"I found this note Azahdi had apparently written to himself." Schneider handed the plastic bag to John. Was there a flicker of recognition? . . .alarm? . . . in John's eye? Schneider couldn't be sure.

"I see."

"Do you know what he was referring to?"

John looked him straight in the eye. "No . . . I haven't the faintest idea."

"John, I want to help you but you have to level with me."

"I believe you . . . Bob. Unfortunately I can't help you."

Schneider sighed. This was getting him nowhere except deeper and deeper in trouble with his superiors if they found out about his new modus operandi. "Okay. Don't tell anyone about this note until Monday. I can sit on it till then."

"Why should you?"

"I don't think you are guilty."

"Don't think so or don't feel so?"

"It amounts to the same thing."

"The result is the same but the process is quite different."

"I'm having a tough time with all this feeling stuff."

"You are bound to at first. You seem to be handling it so far."

"I don't understand it."

"Think of it as a dam. All your emotions were pent up behind it for years. Seeing your mother burst the dam, and the initial flood almost washed you away. Now the stream is free, but it is searching for new channels."

"You're good at analogies, John. Judy was telling me about your ball bearing-marshmallow theory. By the way . . .what am I?"

"It's 'Judy' now." Schneider blushed under John's inquiring gaze. "Anyway, that's easy. You are clearly a steel-jacketed marshmallow that has developed a leak."

"John, I hope I can find something else to go on before Monday. The press has gotten on Goldstein's death, and the legislature is pressing the Governor. I don't want you to be the scapegoat."

"I know. I don't want you to get in trouble either. I appreciate your holding the note. I have to go away this weekend, and I doubt if I could if you brought that out."

"Where are you going?"

"Atlantic City. Randy and I are entered in the Eastern Power Lifting Championships on Saturday."

"Who's Randy?"

"That's right. You haven't met him. He's a resident from the Long Term Care Unit."

"A patient?"

"Sure," laughed John. "Are you surprised?"

"I didn't know patients were allowed off the grounds."

"They go off the grounds all the time, with or without permission. The only thing unusual about this is that the trip is out of state and this is a high level competition."

"Are you that good?"

"Not really. I almost made it to the Nationals once but that was years ago."

"How good is Randy?"

"He might win it. If he could ever get motivated I don't know what he could do. I'm just going along for the ride. I barely qualified in my weight class. Randy's lifts are among the best in the country."

"Is Illanna going along?" A shadow passed across John's face when Schneider mentioned the gypsy . . . or did he just imagine it?

"Yes."

"I'll need an address where you can be reached in case I need to get in touch with you."

John wrote down the name of the motel where they would be staying. "We're going down Friday and should be back late Saturday night."

"Okay. I'll see you on Monday." Schneider left John's office and headed downtown. Six o'clock seemed like a long time away. He couldn't remember the last time he looked forward to anything.

CHAPTER SEVEN -- QUASIMODO

I

John signed Randy out on a weekend pass and drove him home to pick up Illanna and the van. After a quick supper, they sacked out in the back of the van while Illanna made the four hour drive to Atlantic City. They got adjoining rooms at the motel, and Randy was soon snoring again next door.

"Schneider found a note in Azahdi's desk linking Azahdi and Goldstein."

"What was it about?"

"It made reference to something Azahdi had on me."

"What was it?"

"I honestly don't know. Schneider didn't believe me, though. The only thing I can figure out is that he found out about me smuggling you out of there before."

"But how could he? He hadn't been working in the hospital then and had no connection with the Psychiatric Treatment Center, had he?"

"No. But that's not what puzzles me. Why would he need to have something on me? He and Goldstein must have been up to something they thought I could foul up."

"Why didn't Schneider arrest you?"

John laughed. "Schneider's going through a crisis."

"John, that's not funny."

"Not the crisis with his mother."

"What then?"

"He's becoming a human being."

"That's a crisis?"

"It is for Schneider. He's never allowed himself to be dependent upon or to like anyone. Now he suddenly finds himself liking the person he should arrest for murder."

"How is he dealing with that?"

"The way he always deals with things. He's intellectualizing it. He doesn't want to arrest me, so logically it must follow that I am not guilty."

"This is serious, though, John. How long can he avoid arresting you?"

"He's afraid when he shows the note to his superiors on Monday they will order him to arrest me."

"Monday?"

"That's right. He's withholding evidence in his own case."

"He *has* changed!" Illanna was incredulous.

"You don't know how much. He's in love."

"With whom?"

"Judy, the charge nurse in Geriatrics."

"How do you know?"

"All of a sudden he's on a first name basis with her, and he gets that glossy look in his eye when he mentions her."

"What about her?"

"I don't know. I haven't talked to her since he developed the love-sick look. It would be a tragedy if he was totally rejected his first time out. This seems to be the season for puppy love."

"What do you mean?" asked Illanna.

"Didn't you notice the way Randy was mooning over you at dinner?"

"He hardly looked at me!"

"Randy's very shy around girls, but he was smitten with you."

"John, really!"

"No, I'm serious. You will have to be careful around him."

"He wouldn't do anything!"

"Oh, I'm not worried about you."

"Thanks!"

"I mean he can take rejection even less than Schneider."

"So what am I supposed to do? One lummox in my life is quite enough, thank you!"

John laughed. "I'm not matchmaking. Just warning you to treat it as you would any juvenile crush. Firm but gentle."

Illanna became serious. "I'm worried about Monday, John. Is Schneider really going to arrest you?"

"Unless he can come up with something else by then."

"Do you think he will?"

"If he doesn't, maybe we can help him along," said John.

"How?"

"This business with Randy looks promising. The allusion to the devil fits in with Malleus' note and you say that Queenie is into black magic."

"What are we going to do?"

"Well, first let's see if we can get anything out of Randy."

"How?"

"Tomorrow the heavy weight division is in the afternoon. I'll be lifting, and you and Randy will be alone. Maybe you can get him to talk about Queenie."

"Okay."

"I have a hunch who the devil might be, and Sunday you and I will pay him a visit at home."

"Who is it?"

"I won't prejudice you by saying. I'll let you do your thing and see if he is the one you saw in the cards."

"You are starting to believe, aren't you, John?"

"I guess I am, and so are you."

"What am I beginning to believe?" Illanna wondered out loud.

"That all of psychology is not nonsense. We are looking at the same phenomenon from two different sides. I infer feelings and motives from the behavior I see and what people say. You experience them directly."

"You can accept that I do experience them?"

"With great reluctance. All of my training in the scientific method goes against my reasoning from intangibles to tangibles. On the other hand, my training in statistics and probability makes it more difficult to reject your system every time you are right."

"You have great psychic powers yourself, John."

"Then why can't I experience the things you do?"

"I think I know. Psychic powers are not evenly distributed in people. Everyone has them to some extent, but there are different types of abilities. Some people, like me, are receivers. They pick up psychic messages very easily. People like you are senders. I usually know what you are doing, how you are and so forth. It may be that your power of projection actually interferes with your ability to receive."

"Well, in any event I hope your receiver is working on Sunday. I hinted to Johnson that I was onto something. If we don't come up with an alternate to me by Monday, things could get hairy. I'm not going to be able to find Malleus if I'm in jail."

II

The next morning the three of them had a late breakfast and then went for a stroll on the boardwalk. John always got the jitters before a meet.   Randy didn't seem nervous but was extremely withdrawn and self-conscious.   It didn't help that the morning joggers and cyclists all turned to look at them as they went by. They did look like escapees from a side show. Illanna was dressed in her gypsy finest, a print skirt, white blouse and bandanna. Her black ringlets hung below the scarf, framing her black flashing eyes and sharp features. John was sloppy in his Levis and sweatshirt and looked like one of the other participants in a bear wrestling match. Randy received the most attention, though. Bib overalls were about the only thing he could get to fit him. At 5'3" and 275 pounds, he was as wide as John and Illanna put together.   With his short bow legs he rolled like a sailor, and everyone cleared a wide path for him.

They registered at noon, and John went immediately to the warm-up room while Illanna and Randy found seats up close to the lifting stage. As usual there were almost as many lifters as there were people in the audience.   For all of its recent exposure on TV, power lifting still did not draw much of a crowd, even the Eastern Championships.

The light heavy-weights were just starting their final lift, the deadlift. It would be at least an hour before the heavy-weights started. Randy was beginning to come out of himself. Scattered through the audience were the other super heavy-weights. Randy had always been the shortest and widest person in his world. Now he was suddenly thrust into a population where he was almost ordinary. At 275 he was only 25 pounds over the heavy-weight limit. Many of the super heavy-weights were well over 300 pounds. He was still the shortest, but here he looked like a scaled-down version of the rest of the lifters. This had been one of the reasons John had gotten Randy into power lifting – to show him that he was not unique.

Illanna waited until he had gawked around for a while before she tried to draw him out in conversation.

"Randy?"

"Huh?"

"Are you nervous about tonight?"

"Nope."

"Not at all?"

"Dr. John will tell me what to do."

"You like John, don't you?"

"He's my friend."

"I'm your friend too, Randy."

Randy didn't answer.

"Do you have other friends at the Hospital?"

"Nope."

"No one you can talk to?"

"Only Mrs. Slade."

"Oh? Who is she?" Illanna was hating the deceitful way in which she was handling this. She didn't have any choice. John had instructed her to find out about Queenie's relationship with Randy.

"She's the boss."

"Boss of what?"

"Everything . . . Long Term Care."

"Is that where you are?"

"Yes."

This was like pulling teeth. Illanna persisted. "What do you do there?"

"Nothing."

"Nothing? All day, every day?"

"I lift weights with Dr. John."

Illanna decided to take a different tack. "You know, Randy, John's in trouble."

Randy turned sharply to look at her, lines of worry furrowing his craggy face. "What trouble?"

"You know about the two deaths at the hospital, Dr. Azahdi and Senator Goldstein?"

"Yes."

"The police think John did it."

"Dr. John wouldn't . . ."

"We know that, but the police don't."

Illanna hated herself as she watched Randy get more agitated. She wasn't afraid of Randy as most people were. All she saw was a sad child in a man's body. She was forced to use the only joy in his life to get the information they so desperately needed. She continued. "We have to do something to help him."

"What can we do?"

"We can find the person who really did kill them."

"How can we do that?"

"John has an idea, but he needs your help. He thinks it's the Devil who did it."

Randy took in a sharp breath. It was too late to stop now. "John says you know who the Devil is."

"No, I don't."

"But you told John the Devil made you do bad things."

"He does, but I don't . . ." Randy trailed off in confusion.

"Don't what, Randy?"

"I don't know who he is."

"Why not?"

"He wears a mask."

"Then it is a real person?"

"Yes."

"This is very important, Randy. We have to find out who he is. What does he make you do?"

Randy flushed. "I can't tell you."

"Why not?"

"She said Dr. John would get in trouble."

"Who is she?"

"You know."

"Are you talking about Mrs. Slade?"

Randy nodded.

"Why would John get in trouble?"

"I don't know."

Illanna tried to control her impatience. She was so close. "Randy, listen. John is already

in trouble. The only way he can get out is if
we find out who the Devil is. When do you see
him?"

"Different times."

"Where do you see him?"

"I don't know."

Illanna stamped her foot. "Of course you do!"
She got a grip on herself and continued. "You
must know *where* you see him."

"No, I don't. She blindfolds us."

"Us?"

"Me and the others."

"There are others?"

"Yes."

"How many others?"

"I don't know . . . seven?"

"You must have some idea where she takes
you. Where do you start?"

"In the basement of the Center."

"Where in the basement?"

"In the laundry room."

"Where does that lead?"

"Lead?"

"How do you get out of there?"

"The tunnels, I guess."

John had told Illanna about the tunnel system. She knew of its existence but had no concept of how extensive it was. "Where are you when she takes the blindfolds off?"

"In a room."

"What kind of room?"

"A stone room."

"Does the room have any windows?"

"No."

"Is there anything in the room?"

"Only a statue and a table."

Illanna's flesh was beginning to crawl as she pulled out the details of the room. "What is the statue of . . . I mean what does it look like?"

"Him."

"The Devil?"

"Yes."

Illanna was almost afraid to ask the next question because she already knew the answer. "Are there markings on the floor?"

"A funny shaped star."

Illanna took a pad of paper out of her purse and made a hasty drawing. "Does it look like this?"

Randy scratched his head. "I think so."

Illanna shuddered. Randy squirmed, waiting for the inevitable questions about the activities which went on in that room. Illanna was silent. She was beginning to understand the nature of the messages she had been getting from the Hospital.

"Okay, Randy. You don't have to tell me any more."

"Is Dr. John going to get into trouble?"

"I don't think so. What you told me may help him."

"You won't tell Mrs. Slade I told you?" Randy's voice was pleading.

"No, I won't tell her, Randy."

III

The bench press started at three hundred and
seventy-five pounds. At least John isn't the
first to lift, thought Illanna. She knew John's
heart wasn't in this meet. He had been
inactive on the power lifting circuit for several
years before he started working out with
Randy. He had barely qualified for the
Easterns in the last meet he had entered –
Randy's first.

The lead-off contestant handled the weight
easily. No one else started at this weight so
the spotters increased the poundage to 400.
Illanna knew John had planned to start at this
weight. Several other lifters had also chosen
this as the "sure thing." The biggest mistake
you can make in a weight lifting meet is to
choose your first lift too high. If you miss on
all three attempts you are out of the contest
for all practical purposes. You may still win
one of the other two lifts, but there is no way
to make up on the total.

John was the third lifter to go at 400 pounds.
This was not an easy lift for him, but he had
made it several times in practice over the last
few months and he knew he could do more in
a meet with the adrenaline flowing. The
spotters handed the weight to him at arms'
length and he lowered it to his chest. After
the requisite two second pause, the judge

clapped his hands, and John arched out his chest as the weight exploded upwards. He locked out easily and held the weight until the spotters guided the weight back onto the supports.

He stayed out at 415 pounds and made his next attempt at 425. John never made this weight in practice but had made it in several meets. He managed to get it up but his left arm trailed his right and he got two out of three red sticks from the judges signaling a bad lift. He had three minutes to rest before his third and final lift. Illanna was relieved that he had missed his first attempt at 425. She knew it was his record, and if he had made it he would probably have tried something ridiculous for his final lift. Now he still had a chance to tie his record but would not get hurt. John paced back and forth behind the weight, psyching himself up for the lift. Randy was squirming around in his seat, more keyed up for John's lift than he usually was for his own.

Back on the bench, John inhaled sharply as he lowered the weight to his chest. The weight came up slowly but steadily past the sticking point. His left arm seemed to trail slightly behind the right again but it was much more even than the last lift. He locked out. As he sat up he looked over at the judges. Two white sticks. The lights came on the board confirming the good lift.   Randy and Illanna cheered and hugged each other.

John also equaled his past records in the squat and the deadlift, which put him in the top ten. It wasn't a bad finish for a comeback meet.

Randy and Illanna congratulated him when he came out front. Then Randy went back to change and Illanna and John had a few minutes to talk.

"That was terrific, John!"

"Not bad for an old man."

"Does it qualify you for the nationals?"

"Barely, but I was mostly in it to support Randy. I didn't want him to go into his first big meet alone."

"He doesn't seem to be keyed up."

"He never is. He's almost apologetic when he lifts. It's like he's sorry he lifts so much."

"How's he going to do?"

"It's hard to say. He has a shot at the world record in the bench. It's really going to shock these people, because he's an unknown. His other two lifts are a question mark. I don't know what he could do if he got mad. His practice lifts are in it with these guys but not outstanding."

"Are you going back with him?"

"In a few minutes. Did you find out anything?"

"Yes. Queenie has Randy and some other patients in some kind of Devil cult."

John whistled. "Did you find out who the Devil is?"

"Randy doesn't know. He always wears a mask."

"Where do they meet?"

"He doesn't know that either. Queenie leads them to the place blindfolded. It seems to be somewhere down in the tunnel system."

"That fits. Malleus has been using the tunnel system to get around. What goes on at the meetings?"

"That's what worries me, John. I didn't question Randy about that, because I'm sure a lot of the activity is sexual and that seems to be one of Randy's hang-ups. The problem is that they may accomplish what they are setting out to do."

"What do you mean?"

"Conjure up the Devil."

"Oh, come on."

John was beginning to buy the E.S.P. and even take a friendly interest in some aspects of witchcraft, but this was too much.

"Dammit, John, you're always so sure of everything! I'm telling you those people are messing with something they don't understand. Remember? I told you that Queenie was a good technician. From Randy's description of the room she has a classical set-up for conjuring up evil spirits. You combine that with the raw evil power her make-believe devil possesses, and anything can happen."

John wasn't going to get sucked into their usual confrontation again. "Okay, but our immediate concern is finding out the identity of the Devil they have already conjured up."

"You said you might know who that was."

"I know Rachel. She does nothing for nothing. If she is involved in something like this, she has to be getting something out of it for herself. There are not too many people in the hospital who can do anything for her. She is pretty far up on the ladder."

"What do we do next?"

"First we get Randy through the meet. Then tomorrow we go on a picnic."

IV

Back stage the behemoths were finishing their
warm up. The mammoth bodies looked like
beached whales sweating in the sun. John
and Randy were in a corner with no one
paying much attention to them. All of the
other lifters were familiar with each other.
They competed regularly in the open meets
and regional championships. Randy was an
unknown and because of his small size
relative to the others, hardly noticed.

The super-heavy-weights started benching
where the heavyweights had left off at 550
pounds. One after the other they dropped out
as the weight crept closer to the world record,
750 pounds. Only one of the lifters was
considered a threat to it. George Marsh, a
giant from the New England area had come
within 10 pounds several times in open
competition. It was rumored that he had
broken it in practice but one always had to
take such rumors with a grain of salt.   March
took his first lift at 700 pounds. Two other
lifters failed on their third attempt, leaving
March the only lifter. He made the lift easily.
At 725 pounds he had more difficulty but he
got two white sticks and asked for 750
pounds as his last attempt. The crowd was
disappointed that he had not requested a
weight over the record. It turned out,
however, that Marsh knew his limitations and

never got the bar off his chest. The crowd sat back in anticipation of the squat. Suddenly a buzz started in the first row and spread quickly throughout the auditorium. They were not clearing the bench away. One lifter had not taken his first lift! Randy waddled up the steps and positioned himself on the bench. He was not thinking about the lift or the weight. He was thinking about all those people out there . . . people he could not see because of the stage lights . . . people gawking at his massive misshapen body. The weight came crashing down out of control. The spotters grabbed the weight as fast as they could, but not before there was a sickening snap that could be heard all over the auditorium. The audience groaned. They had seen it all before. The newcomer, in over his head, trying an impossible weight to stay in the competition, the inevitable injury.

Two other lifters had to assist in getting the ponderous weight back onto the supports. John and the attending physician helped Randy off the stage. The head judge walked after them to get the official confirmation that Randy was out of the competition. The audience watched the tableau with increasing interest. The buzz started again as they saw the judge looking at the time lapse clock. The straps were down on Randy's lifting suit and the doctor was using the better part of a roll of adhesive tape trying to get around Randy's chest. John was talking to Randy excitedly. "Are you sure you want to go on?"

"Yes."

"Your rib might be broken."

"It don't hurt much."

"But if it is and you lose the weight again you could be seriously hurt."

"I won't lose it."

"What happened before?"

"I wasn't ready for it."

"Okay. This time get mad at it! Start now! The weight wants to hurt you, to punish you, to humiliate you in front of all the people. Are you going to let the weight do that to you?"

"No."

"I can't hear you, Randy."

"No!" Randy yelled and the doctor almost fell over backwards. Two minutes had elapsed and Randy waddled up the stairs again. The audience sat in shocked silence.

This time the breath whistled through Randy's teeth as the spotters handed him the weight. Instead of crashing down on his chest the weight settled down slowly until it rested on the bindings. When the signal sounded the weight started to move, not in an explosion but in an inevitable climb. The lift was never in doubt. Slowly but steadily the bar moved past the sticking point. A roaring crescendo came from the audience cheering the lift when it was only half over. Randy locked out and held the weight steady until the spotters guided it back to the supports. The place went crazy. John helped Randy, who was obviously in pain, off the bench. "Maybe we better call it quits."

"Naw, that wasn't too bad."

"Does your chest hurt?"

"Some, but if I let the weight down slowly, it's alright."

"It doesn't bother you on the way up?"

"Not after it's off my chest. Not until they take it."

"What do you want to do? You only have to increase the weight five pounds for a new world record."

"I can do 775."

"Are you sure?"

"Yes."

"Okay. You need the cushion. The sequel is going to be hell on that rib."

The head judge announced the next weight was 775 pounds. The crowd was numb. Twenty-five pounds over the world record, an unknown, injured lifter was making the attempt. Illanna wrung her hands nervously. Four spotters, instead of the usual two, stood by. Randy waddled up the stairs again. A low chanting sound began to build in the audience. "Randy . . . Randy . . . Randy . . . Randy."

He assumed the position, and the spotters handed him the weight. Again he inched it down to his chest. When the signal started, it seemed for an instant that was where it was going to stay. Then daylight appeared between the bandages and the bar. The weight came up even slower than it had before but just as inevitably. The crowd continued to chant, and the chant seemed to get under the bar. "Randy . . . Randy . . .Randy," pushing it past the sticking point. Everyone was on their feet screaming when he locked out. The judges had to declare it a good lift or they never would have gotten out of the auditorium alive.

John helped Randy off the bench and supported him down off the platform. "How are the ribs?"

"They hurt now but not while I'm lifting."

"That's when the pressure is on them. You better do some practice squats before we decide what to do next."

John and Randy went back to the warm-up room. Randy took a few practice lifts with 500 pounds, a relatively light weight for his division. He winced each time he passed the sticking point.

"Are you going to be able to do a heavy lift?"

"I don't know. It hurts in the middle of the lift going down and coming up."

"That's when the pressure goes on the ribs and comes off. The question is whether you will be able to stand the pain with a really heavy lift."

"I don't know. I think so."

John decided the best thing was to go for a medium lift. If Randy failed at that, it was academic as far as his chances for the overall championship. If he made it with no difficulty he could go on to a heavy lift. If he had to stop with the one lift he still had a chance if he could get in a good deadlift. He outlined the strategy to Randy and then went out to talk to Illanna.

"John, that was unbelievable!"

"I told you. Imagine what he could do if he wasn't hurt."

"Is he going to be able to do the squat and the deadlift?"

"We have to take it one at a time. It hurt for him to do the squat, but he handled 500 pounds okay. There's no way to tell if he is going to be able to handle the real poundage without trying it. There's no sense doing that in a practice lift. He's going to wait it out until it gets around 900 pounds and see how it goes."

"What has he done in practice?"

"His best is 990."

"Is that good?"

"It's competitive with the national champions, but it's not world record."

Most of the audience was looking at John and Illanna. No one had paid much attention to them before, but the drama of the bench press had made them the center of attention. Speculation about the extent of Randy's injury and his ability to go on was primary.

The announcer gave the last call for the squat, and John returned to the warm-up room. Randy was talking to the physician. When John approached, the doctor turned to him."

"Ah-hem."

"Dr. Lowell." John introduced himself.

"Yes, Doctor. I can't determine whether the ribs are cracked or just bruised."

"You don't think they are broken?"

"No. They are painful when I push, but they don't move around."

"Is it safe for him to do the squat?"

"It's safe enough, but he may pass out from the pain."

"Okay. Then we are going to risk it. I didn't want Randy to puncture a lung or something."

"There's no danger of that."

"Tell the judges we are going to continue, then."

The squat started at 700 pounds, the qualifying weight for the Eastern Championship. Randy lay on his back resting on the mat. John stood in the wings of the stage watching the early contestants.

The bench press had gotten Marsh's attention.. He sat in a corner of the warm-up room, trying to avoid looking in Randy's direction. But trying not to look at something is like trying not to blink. Eventually you succumb. Randy, on the other hand, was completely oblivious to Marsh. It was not within Randy's scope to consider beating anyone at anything. His world was filled with jumbled thoughts and feelings. He was trying to sort out the feelings he got when the crowds cheered him. The cheers were so contradictory to his perception of the world . . . a world he had thought could only laugh at him.

Marsh was used to the psyching game. Generally he was in control. Suddenly he was psyched out. Randy had blindsided him from the start. He didn't even know of Randy's existence coming into the meet. All of a sudden he had been blown away by an unknown. Marsh was used to the spotlight and now it was on someone else. He took some comfort from the fact that Randy was hurting. Also, Marsh was competitive in all three lifts . . . unlike some of the "specialists." Randy's injury had to affect his performance in the squat and the deadlift. What was driving Marsh crazy was his total ignorance of what Randy could be expected to do in the remaining lifts. The essence of the game in lifting is to cause the other lifters to start too low or too high. If they start too low, they waste one or two lifts and have to jump too far to make their top weight. If they start too high, they can waste a lift or better yet fail on all three attempts. In order to play the game effectively, though, you have to have a fairly realistic idea of the capabilities of the other lifters. Marsh had zero information.

Randy wouldn't be psyched out by what
Marsh did, because he was unaware of
Marsh's existence. Without trying, Randy was
engaging in the perfect play to upset his major
competitor. Marsh had been treated in many
ways but never ignored. The object of the
game is to get the other competitor to think
about you instead of the lift . . . to break his
concentration. Randy had succeeded with
Marsh.

Marsh decided to start low and draw Randy
out. The crowd was surprised when he was
announced at 800 pounds. They expected
him to push 1000. He made the lift easily and
waited to see Randy's move. Randy didn't. At
850 pounds, John came over and talked to
Randy, and Marsh saw Randy shake his head.
Marsh was determined not to waste another
lift, so he waited him out. At 875 pounds
John walked over and spoke to the announcer.
Randy had decided to try 900 pounds. It was
less than his best lift in practice but still not
an easy lift for him even without the injury.
All Marsh knew was that this was his starting
weight.

Randy shrugged out of his warm-up suit.
Black and blue patches had begun to peek out
from beneath the bandages around his ribs.
No chanting this time. He ducked beneath the
bar, settling it on the bulge of the trapezius
muscle behind his neck. He groaned as he

straightened beneath the bar. The spring steel bowed, and the weight cleared the supports. He shuffled two steps forward and paused. The starter signaled his okay. Randy took three quick breaths and started down. Halfway into the squat, an involuntary groan was wrenched from him as the weight pressed his ribs down against his bulging midsection. The spotters took a step toward him, but he didn't lose the weight. He descended slowly till his thighs were parallel with the floor and then below parallel. For a split second John thought he had gone too low, but Randy came out of it and the weight began to rise. He passed the sticking point with no problem, but when he was almost up, the pressure came off his ribs and another cry was torn from him. He swayed at the top but held the weight for the prescribed time and staggered back with it, as the spotters guided it onto the rack. The color drained from his face, and he fell backwards onto the stage.

John and the doctor rushed out on the stage as the judges lifted the three white sticks, signaling a good lift. The crowd did not applaud the lift but were on their feet craning to see if Randy was all right. The doctor cracked an ammonia cap under Randy's nose, and he was soon conscious. He winced as they helped him off the stage.

"Are you all right?" John's voice came through the red haze of Randy's pain.

"Yeah. What happened?"

"You fainted."

"What about the lift?"

"It was a good lift."

"I don't think I can do another one."

"You don't have to. Do you want to call it quits or try a deadlift?"

"I don't think the deadlift will bother me much if I don't wear the belt."

"Rest for a few minutes and we'll try it."

Randy went back to the mat in the corner and lay down. Marsh had been trying to edge close enough to find out what was going on but only heard the last sentence. "How is he?"

John took a long look at him before replying. "He's fine."

"Is he going to keep lifting?"

"Why not?"

Marsh turned and walked away. He checked with the announcer. He didn't believe Randy could do another weight. His original plan had been to start at 900, do his second lift at 950, and depending upon how he felt go to 975 or 1000 pounds. He checked in for 950 to

make up for the 50 pound deficit in the bench
press. Marsh had miscalculated. His first lift
at 800 pounds was really only a warm-up
weight for him. When he took the 950
pounds it seemed like the weight of the world
on his shoulders. The seeds of doubt planted
in his mind during the bench press were
blossoming into a fear of losing. The weight
drove him down past the parallel point into a
full squat and there he stayed.

The crowd was stunned again. They expected
him to make the weight easily. There were
scattered cat calls. Marsh's popularity had
vanished. The crowd's fickle support was
now totally for Randy.   Marsh walked
disgustedly to the side and tried to get it
together for his final attempt at 950. Stung by
the lack of support from the crowd, the
psychology of the situation began to work in
his favor. His pride was hurt, and he began to
get angry. By the time the three minute clock
signaled it was time for his lift, he had worked
himself into a pretty good rage. It didn't
matter what he was mad at – he took it out on
the weight. This time he made the lift with no
problem. He walked, at least partially
vindicated, off the stage dead even with Randy
for the two lifts.

The contest was down to the deadlift, which
was frequently the case.   Most lifters could
handle the greater poundages of the deadlift or

they wouldn't be at this level. Because of the enormous weights, however, the spread of lifts was also the greatest. In most cases the overall competition was decided by the man who could deadlift the most.

As in all weightlifting events, the crowd is turned on most by the absolute amount of weight lifted. This favors the super heavy weight class, and within this class the deadlift, which is the last lift. The crowd, composed mainly of friends and relatives of the lifters, was experienced and knowledgeable, but had never seen drama compared to that which was unfolding before them now. Randy, the emotional favorite, was obviously hurting. His single lift in the squat demonstrated his reduced ability. On the other hand, rib injuries were not as problematic in the deadlift as they were in the squat.

Marsh was back in the same quandary that he had been in when the squat began. He had no idea when Randy would start to lift. He was determined not to make the same mistake in the deadlift he had made before.

He decided to stick to his original plan, which was to make a 1000 pound deadlift, an easy one for him, jump to 1100, and if he made that, try for 1200. He knew he had to beat Randy. A tie would automatically go to the lighter lifter. The deadlift started at 750 pounds. One by one, the other lifters dropped out as the weight approached the half ten mark. As before, Randy still had not made his first lift.

John sat next to him, his back to the cinderblock wall, while Randy lay flat on the mat. "Do you want to take some warm-up lifts?"

"No."

"You sure?"

"Yeah. Either I can do it or I can't. I may only be able to make one lift like before."

"What weight do you want to start at?"

"Around 1000. Depends on Marsh."

John was amazed. Randy had never shown any sign of competition before, at least not competition against another person. "You really want to beat him, don't you?"

"No. But I want to win."

"Why?"

"Because they want me to." Randy gestured toward the auditorium.

John was pleased. Randy had come a long way. His recognition of the crowd's support was the first time he had admitted the possibility that the world was not entirely hostile and that others could have some positive regard for him. It was a good beginning but only that. Eventually the feelings of self-worth had to come from inside. If Randy was ever to approach his potential as a human being, he had to rise above his looking glass self. John vowed to himself that he would never allow Randy to take a backward step into the world of defeatism and self-pity. "What do you think you can deadlift?"

"I don't know."

"You've never done anything over 1000 pounds in practice."

"I know."

"Were you trying?"

"I thought I was, but now . . . "

"You're not sure you were doing your best?"

"No."

"I'm not sure either, Randy. I don't know what your best is, but I have a feeling, and have had for some time, that it is something awesome."

Randy was silent. Marsh was talking to the announcer. John looked at the board. 1000 pounds was coming up."

"You want me to make it 1000."

"Yeah."

John went over to the announcer and saw
Marsh's name next to the 1000 pound mark.
He signed Randy up. The two remaining
lifters were both going to attempt 1000 as the
third lift. They tried and failed.

Marsh had his confidence back. 1000 pounds
was an easy lift for him. So far his plan was
working. Randy was also slated to start at
1000. 100 pound jumps were not usual.
With Randy's injury it was doubtful he could
make the first jump to 1100. Marsh knew he
could. Marsh's only remaining worry was the
possibility of a tie which would go to Randy.

The crowd applauded as Marsh walked onto
the platform. He was still popular, and the
crowd was enjoying the battle between the
veteran and the newcomer. Marsh chalked his
hands and stood for a moment in
concentration over the bar. Then he leaned
over into a half squat and pulled. The
ponderous weight came up easily, and he
leaned back at the top waiting for the judge's
signal. It was a good lift. The crowd
applauded politely. They knew this was far
below Marsh's potential.

Randy received a warmer reception. The
crowd had no idea what he would do in the
deadlift. His injury was still a question mark.
In some ways, Randy was built ideally for this

lift. His short legs should have meant that he didn't have to go below parallel with his legs. On the other hand, his short arms, an advantage in the bench press, meant he had to bend over farther to grip the bar. On balance, his build neither favored nor worked against him. He stood over the bar psyching himself up. Randy's shoulders were so wide they seemed to go from collar to collar on the wide Olympic bar. His hands fell naturally to the outside portion of the knurling on the bar. He reversed his grip on the right to keep the bar from rolling and pulled. The pain in his chest wrenched a cry from him halfway through the lift, but the weight came up evenly and he got three white sticks from the judges. John helped him down the steps.

"How was it?"

"Not as bad as the squat."

"What do you want next?"

"I'll go with Marsh."

"You're already at your record."

"I can do more."

Marsh was encouraged by Randy's exclamation of pain during the lift. His plan seemed to be working. He signed up for 1100 pounds. John conferred with Randy again.

"He's going for 1100."

"Okay."

"You're sure you don't want 1050?"

"No, I want the last lift."

Marsh was ecstatic. Randy was falling into the trap. He might conceivably make the first 100 pound jump, but no way the second with that injury. The lift was announced, and Marsh ascended the platform. The crowd was restive. This was still well below Marsh's best lift. He made the weight easily, and there was scattered polite applause. The applause crescendoed as Randy rolled up the steps for the same weight. He stared for a minute at the weight and then up at the ceiling as if in supplication.

This time he bent down quickly and grabbed the bar, pulling immediately. The bar bent so much with the quick action that Randy was halfway up before the weights cleared the floor. When Randy was in an upright position the weights caught up with the bar, and the momentum took them past parallel, lifting him onto his toes. There was a stunned silence for a split second and then the crowd exploded. They had never seen, nor would probably ever see again, a lift like that. Those of the crowd who also followed Olympic lifting recognized the first half of the clean in getting the weight to the shoulders, but that was done with less than half the weight that was on that bar.

Marsh was badly shaken. He had been nationally ranked for ten years on the powerlifting circuit and had never seen really heavy poundage handled like that. The judges were conferring. The lift was so unexpected that they had to check with each other to be sure no rules had been broken. None had. The three white sticks went up, and the white lights followed on the board. The cheers went up again.

John shook his head in amazement. "Randy, that was terrific. Why did you lift it that way?"

"I don't know. I wasn't thinking about it."

"What were you thinking about?"

"I just pictured the weight being up and went for it."

"You looked like you could have cleaned it."

"Not with a reverse grip," Randy laughed.

"I know," smiled John, "but that snapping technique is something you see in Olympic lifts. You're not supposed to be able to do it with this kind of weight."

Marsh looked like a loser when he signed up for 1200 pounds. He didn't know what he was doing any more. Randy didn't follow any of the patterns he had seen in other meets. If his last lift was an indication, Randy could deadlift a ton. Marsh saw John conferring with Randy for the last lift. He expected him to sign up for the same weight. A tie would go to Randy. "You want 1200?"

"No."

"What, then?"

"1250."

"Why? 1200 will win it even if he makes it."

"I don't want to win that way."

"You got away with it last time, but your injury may catch up with you."

"I can do it."

John put Randy's name next to 1250. Marsh was too numb to take heart from the tactical error. He tried desperately to get it together for the lift. He reached back into his years of experience, blocking everything out of his mind except the weight. Experience paid off. He made the lift with only a slight hitch in the middle. He got two white sticks, a good lift. He was done. Now it was up to Randy. He was almost pulling for the young, game lifter.

Randy waddled up to the bar. There was a hushed silence in the auditorium. Emotions were drained. In contrast to the last lift, Randy settled slowly to the bar. As he gripped it he seemed to expand. The veins in his hands and forearms popped to the surface, his shoulders sagged against the guying support of the trapezius muscles. He threw his head back against the cords of his neck and began to pull. It was a slow motion repeat of his previous lift. The weight came up slowly, inevitably. It was a perfect lift.

Already hoarse, the crowd too made a last effort and brought down the rafters. Randy had won. No one other than John knew how much he had won. John knew. Illanna felt the quality of the victory. Not the victory of man over weight or man over man but man over himself.

On the ride home, Randy slept in the back of the van, his arm around the enormous trophy.

"He's something, isn't he John?"

"He's pretty special. I think this is a turning point for Randy. He's going to be alright."

"This is what you hoped for?"

"It's more than I had hoped for or dreamed of. I have always known Randy had the potential to be a good lifter. I wasn't sure whether he could conquer his own self-doubts. He can and did."

Illanna nestled against the psychologist's shoulder sleepily. "I love you, John."

It was after three o'clock in the morning when the van pulled in front of the Long Term Building. The third shift charge nurse looked curiously at the trio as they entered the lobby. "What's going on?"

"Randy won the Eastern Powerlifting Championship."

"Oh?" The charge nurse didn't say, "What's that?", but the inflection was there. John didn't care. It wasn't for the rest of the world. It was for Randy, and no one could take it away from him. They took Randy up to his room. The charge nurse dialed an outside number.

CHAPTER EIGHT -- QUEENIE

I

The river swept down into the fish weir and then broadened out again around the islands in the main channel. Wild water frothing through the last gorge of the Appalachians settled into the turgid river which flowed through the Pennsylvania Dutch farmlands of Lancaster County. Here, in the foothills of the ancient mountains, rhododendron, mountain laurel, and hemlocks bent over the banks shading the swift water.

John pulled off the main road onto a well rutted dirt track, which led precipitously down to a break in the underbrush and a small beach landing.

He unlashed the canoe from the top of the van and slid it onto his shoulders, the center thwart resting snugly in the fold of the muscle behind his neck. He hurried with an Indian portage shuffle down to the sandy strip and expertly rolled the canoe down onto his knees before sliding it into the water. Illanna brought the picnic basket and paddles from the van, and they were soon pushing out into the main current.

It was hard work paddling against the swift water, but John had purposely "put in" below their destination so that they could get back in a hurry if they had to.

Canoeing had been a life-long passion of John's. He had learned the skills from a Maine guide in his youth. The easy rhythm of his stroke belied the effort it took to counteract the power of the river. He leaned into each stroke and, with Illanna pulling hard in the bow, slowly worked the canoe upstream to the first island below the rocky weir. On the down-stream portion of the island, the current eddied into a small rocky inlet with a few feet of sand to beach the canoe.

"This is beautiful, John."

"Not too many people come up here. It's too rocky for power boats and too much work for canoeists."

"Have you been here often?" A dangerous glint had come into Illanna's eyes.

"Yes . . . fishing." John answered the masked question.

Illana laughed. "It's silly to be jealous."

"A lot of feelings are silly if you look at them rationally. "

"I don't look at them rationally."

"Lord, don't I know it," said John.

"You do."

"I used to."

"You still do."

"I'm trying, but it's getting harder all the time."

Illanna spread the blanket out and unpacked the basket. John ate ravenously. He had had nothing but coffee since the two o'clock hamburgers on the way back from the meet, and it was already late afternoon. As the shadows lengthened, John took out his binoculars and studied the east shore of the river. "I can't see his cabin from here, but he might be able to see the canoe if he was looking."

"Who?" Illanna queried.

"You tell me."

"Stop being mysterious, John. Why are we here and what do you want me to do?"

"I want you to tell me if you feel the presence of our devil."

Illanna picked out a flat rock and sat cross-legged facing the east shore.

She closed her eyes and began to rock slowly back and forth. She began humming the now familiar tune. This time it only took a few minutes.

""They're both here."

"Fortunado and Rachel?"

"Rachel and the evil one . . . Is that his name?"

"Dick Fortunado. He has a cabin over there."
John pointed halfway up the ridge that ran
along the east bank of the river.

"Is he the one you thought was playing the
devil?"

"Once I knew Rachel was involved it didn't
take much of a guess. He and Rachel are
thick as thieves. Fortunado's one of the few
people in the Hospital above her in the
hierarchy. This cult stuff gives her something
on him. She is very ambitious . . . I'm sure
she is making full use of this to manipulate
Dick."

"There's more."

"More what?"

"I didn't just feel their presence."

"What do you mean?"

"They are up to something."

"What kind of something?"

"Ritual witchcraft."

"More conjuring?"

"No. Fortunado is relatively passive. Rachel is
the active one."

John shook his head. "You're amazing."

"Why?"

"You always provide more detail than I ask for. The safe thing to do is just answer my question. It's the law of parsimony."

"What's that?!" Illanna laughed.

"It's a principle of theory-building. You always stick to the simplest explanation because there are fewer chances of being wrong."

"I'm not afraid of being wrong. I just tell you what I feel."

"But that's just what is so amazing. You don't feel any pressure to prove that you are right."

"If *I* didn't believe, I couldn't do what I just did. Whether you believe it or not doesn't matter."

"Well, if you are right, they are too busy to be watching the river, so we can get on over there and check it out."

John backed the canoe out into the river and then sculled across the swift current into the shelter of the east arm of the weir. A couple of minutes of easy paddling brought them into the shore a mile above the beach where they had put in. The rhododendron was thick all along the bank, and they had to duck under the overhanging branches to get to the shore. They left the canoe tethered to one of the giant shrubs and began the steep ascent toward the spot where John had calculated the cabin ought to be. After a few minutes of hard climbing a clearing appeared off to the right.

"They *are* both here," John whispered.

"Are you sure?"

"That's Fortunado's Jeep and the car behind it is Rachel's."

"Should we go closer?"

"We have to be careful. Fortunado's got two Dobermans."

They crept up to the back of the cabin and peered through the kitchen window. The place seemed deserted. Then they heard a dog bark somewhere at a distance up river.

"Let's go."

The hillside banking steeply down to the river was thickly wooded. They crossed the face of it, holding on to saplings to keep from sliding down hill. Soon the river curved off to the west, and they were climbing again up to the top of the ridge. John signaled silence as they neared the edge. A hollow opened up below them cut into the face of the mountain. Giant sycamore trees canopied this ancient place. Looking down through the branches a hundred feet from the bottom of the bowl, Illanna gasped and John put his hand over her mouth.

"Sh!"

Far below them in the gathering twilight Rachel danced naked around a fire.

Fortunado lay on a blanket, half propped up against an old gnarled tree hollowed out from an old wound big enough for several people to walk around in it. The two Dobermans flanked him sniffing the air, their ears cocking back and forth, eyes glinting in the flickering firelight.

"What's she doing?"

"Quit salivating."

"I'm not."

"You bet."

"Come on, Illanna, this is serious. What's she up to?"

Illanna closed her eyes and concentrated. "She's trying to contact me."

"You're kidding!"

"No, she must have felt my probe from the island."

"What should we do?"

Before Illanna could whisper an answer, events decided themselves.

Suddenly Rachel screamed and pointed straight at them. The dogs leapt forward and Fortunado was up in an instant. John reacted almost as quickly.

He wasn't afraid of Fortunado, but the dogs were another matter. He grabbed Illanna's hand and dragged her to her feet. As he turned he saw Fortunado looking straight up at him.

"Come on!"

They began running back toward the canoe. Rocks slipped out from under their feet as they leapt from tree to tree down the face of the steep incline. In less than a minute they were down on the flat stretch next to the river but still some distance from where the canoe was tied. John heard the dogs' running barks coming closer and closer. As he ran he spotted a stout branch and scooped it up. He let Illanna get several yards in front of him and then he stopped and turned. The dogs were up to him in seconds. Teeth bared, the first one leapt for his throat. He swung the cudgel as hard as he could and caught the dog in midair. The dog yelped and swung around. It slammed into a tree and slid down to the base in a heap. The second dog attached himself to John's trouser leg and ripped it to the knee. John brought the club down on his head and he dropped like a stone.

Illanna came up breathlessly behind him. The whole encounter hadn't taken ten seconds. "Are you all right?"

"I'm all right. They aren't."

Both dogs were breathing but out cold. The one at the base of the tree was lying in a funny position.

"That one might have some bones broken."

"You couldn't help it, John. They would have killed you."

"I know. We better get going. I don't want to confront Fortunado just yet."

"Do you think he recognized you?"

"I don't know. He saw me, but my back was to the light and it's getting pretty dark anyway."

They began running again, but this time there was no urgency. Even if Fortunado had come right after them he had to be several minutes behind them. As they rounded the bend in the river they saw the fish weir and the canoe tethered comfortably under the rhododendrons. In a minute they were gliding down river, John adding momentum to the strong current. In five minutes they were back at the landing and in ten back on the road to town.

"What are you going to do now?"

"Tomorrow morning I'm going to blow the whistle on Fortunado and Rachel. Let's see how they like being on the hot seat for a while."

II

"You are under arrest. You have the right to remain silent . . ."

Schneider read John his rights from a card he kept in his wallet.

"Come on, Schneider. Lighten up."

"I'm sorry, Dr. Lowell. I am under instructions to bring you down to headquarters."

"But I have new information."

"What is it?"

"Dr. Richard Fortunado and Mrs. Rachel Slade are operating a devil's cult with some of the patients. It could link up with Malleus."

"Dr. Fortunado has already contacted us. He said you might concoct something to that effect."

"Really! And how would he know what kind of a story I would tell if there weren't some truth in it?"

"He said a patient you had been working with was spreading such a story around."

A sickening feeling was beginning in the pit of John's stomach. "What patient?"

"Randy Stoltzfoos."

"I want to talk to him."

"You can't."

"Why not?"

"He's under heavy sedation."

"Under whose orders?"

"The Superintendent."

"Come on. Johnson doesn't even carry a caseload here. Why would he put Randy under sedation?"

"Apparently Randy became violent shortly after you brought him back from the weight lifting meet."

John's concern for his own predicament was rapidly being replaced by a growing concern for Randy. "That's ridiculous. When we left him early Sunday morning he was fine. In fact I doubt if he ever had a better day in his life either experientially or therapeutically."

"Nevertheless he attacked a nurse and almost killed him."

"I don't believe it."

"It's well documented in the record. Several people had to pull him off. In fact, it took most of the male staff on third shift to bring him under control. He wrecked a good portion of the Long Term Care Building."

"If it's true, someone must have provoked him."

"They said something about a trophy."

John was beginning to understand. "What about the trophy?"

"The nurse tried to confiscate it."

"Why?"

"She said it could be used as a weapon."

"So that's it."

John could just see it. After he and Illanna had left, the building supervisor must have tried to take the trophy from Randy. Randy's resistance was entirely understandable. He had been off lithium for months because of the weight lifting meets. A rage reaction must have been triggered.

"Is Randy all right now? Can I see him?"

"I'm afraid not . . . You are under arrest."

"But Randy can clear this whole thing up."

"Not in his present state. Not in any state really. I doubt if anything he said would be admissible in a court of law."

"But dammit, Schneider. I didn't have anything to do with this, and now they've zonked the only person who can say what's really going on."

"I'm sorry, John. The chief said to have you down at the station this morning and that's what I have to do."

The regret in Schneider's voice was genuine, but so was the determination. He had held out as long as he could. There were no more options. He motioned the two uniformed patrolmen in from the hall. One of them handcuffed John.

"Are these really necessary?"

"It's procedure." Schneider couldn't hold John's eyes.

"Can I make a phone call?"

"Down at the station."

They led John past the nursing station where Judy was crying quietly. Schneider tried to give her a reassuring smile, but Judy looked away. Schneider had never been so miserable. He still didn't believe John was guilty, couldn't believe it. No one spoke in the car, John and the detective each deep in their own thoughts.

The county jail was an ancient brick structure dating back to the early 1800's. It was one of Lancaster's historical landmarks, having served every function in county government at one time or another. During his arrest procedure John was allowed to make his phone call and he called Illanna. He outlined the problem with Randy and was trying to convince her to stay away from the jail and send a lawyer over, but she insisted on coming down. She arrived twenty minutes later but wasn't allowed to see John until he had been fingerprinted and outfitted in the traditional prison denim. She sat across from him in the visiting room, the low screen between them, trying to fight back the tears.

"John, what are you going to do?"

"I don't know. You're going to have to get a lawyer."

"Can he get the hospital to let me see Randy?"

"I don't want you going near the hospital. You shouldn't have come here. If they start looking into your past, and they may have already started, they could send you back to the hospital."

"But I can't just sit home and do nothing."

"No. You can't even sit home. I want you to move out and call me when you get settled."

"Won't that look suspicious?"

"It doesn't matter how suspicious it looks. It's bad enough with one of us locked up. You won't be able to help me if you're in the hospital and I won't be able to help you if you're in there either."

Illanna shuddered, remembering the last time she was behind the iron gates. As they discussed which lawyer to contact, they were being observed from behind a one-way mirror by Schneider and Johnson. Schneider had called Johnson to inform him of the arrest. Johnson asked if he could come down to the station and check something out.

"What did Fortunado tell you?"

"He said that he thought the name Romanowsky was familiar. She seemed familiar to me also when I was at your place." Schneider looked away and Johnson passed over the experience quickly. "Anyway, we went back through the records and there was an Illanna Romanowsky who was court-committed a couple of years ago."

"What happened to her?"

"She escaped."

"Escaped!"

"Yes, after only a couple of days. The disturbing part is that we thought at the time she had to have staff help to get out because she left a locked ward between shifts. Whoever helped her had a key and knew the ward routine well."

"You think John helped her?"

"It's a strong possibility. He was insisting that she be moved off the ward at the time."

"Why?"

"I'd rather not go into that."

"More clinical secrets?"

"Not in this instance, but it's a can of worms I wasn't able to deal with at the time and I don't want to dredge it up now. "

"Is she the woman?"

Johnson looked narrowly at Illanna. "I only saw her at the court hearing, and it was couple of years ago. However, she is a very striking woman and I'm almost positive she is the one. Also it's a very unusual name, and the names are certainly the same."

"What do you want me to do?"

"I don't have any choice. She will have to be returned to the hospital. She is still technically in violation of the court commitment."

"John's going to take this hard."

"It can't be helped. Anyway, you must have some questions you want to ask her yourself. She will be available if she is at the hospital."

Schneider shrugged resignedly and motioned for two guards who were standing by the door.

"We have to make another collar in there."

The two guards looked at each other puzzledly. Both of them had had the duty many times but had never been involved in an arrest in the visiting room.

Schneider continued, "The woman talking to the prisoner at the end is an escapee from the State Hospital. This is the Superintendent, Dr. Johnson. He will be taking her back."

When the three of them were ten feet from John and Illanna, Schneider saw his mistake. He should have waited until Illanna left the room and got her outside. John took one look at the advancing trio and panicked.

"Illanna, get out!"

As Illanna ran for the door, one of the guards reached out and grabbed her. John let out a heartbreaking sob and stood up, grabbing the underside of the partition separating the visitors from the prisoners. The bolted table came out of the floor with a loud grinding snap and the frenzied psychologist threw it aside as if the heavy oak was balsa wood. He charged at the patrolman restraining Illanna. The other officer started to raise his pump gun, but Schneider pushed it aside, drawing his own 38. As John charged by him, he spun the gun around in his hand and clipped him neatly behind the ear. John went down like a poleaxed steer.

Schneider led Illanna, sobbing, into the outer chamber while the two patrolmen dragged John down to the infirmary.

"Schneider, how could you, after John . . "

she trailed off into broken sobs.

"I couldn't have him shot." The words were wrenched out of him. He didn't owe them anything. John was probably a murderer, and Illanna was an escapee from a looney bin. The rationale rang hollow in his mind. He fought to hold back the newly acquired feelings. What would John think . . . think of him? He couldn't pursue that line of thought. "Do you need help in getting her back to the hospital, Doctor?"

Illanna looked at the two of them, terror beginning to get hold of her. "I'm not going back there!"

Johnson's voice was kindly but firm. "I'm afraid you have no choice, Miss Romanowsky."

"I can't go back there!"

"Don't worry. There won't be a repeat of the problems you encountered last time."

"But John . . ."

"Won't be there to help you this time. He was the one who got you out, wasn't he?"

Illanna set her mouth hard and glared at him.

"I want to talk to a lawyer."

"All in good time . . . you are already court-committed to the hospital and have to go back there first."

Illanna hung her head. Schneider spoke to Johnson. "Do you need any help taking her back?"

"Our regulations require female staff to accompany female patients . . . I can have a nurse sent down from the hospital."

"Don't bother. I'll send a female bailiff up and she can come back with one of my men."

Schneider called downstairs, and five minutes later a bailiff appeared.

She produced a set of handcuffs. This time Johnson protested.

"Are those necessary?"

"We have regulations also." Schneider turned away as Illanna was handcuffed and led downstairs.

Illanna was silent for the first couple of minutes in the car. When she spoke, it was not about her predicament.

"You know John isn't guilty."

"I would like to believe that," said Johnson.

"John couldn't hurt anyone."

"Are we talking about the same person who just ripped a visiting room apart?"

"That was to protect me."

"Precisely. Anyone is capable of violence under the proper circumstances."

"But John is incapable of cold-blooded murder."

"I have been in this racket for over forty years, and I don't know yet what anyone is or is not capable of."

"If you lock me up, I am not going to be able to help John clear himself."

"I understand your concern for John, but you had better start considering your own situation."

"I'm not crazy."

"We don't use those terms."

"Mentally disabled, then. Do I seem mentally disabled to you?"

"Frankly, I don't diagnose in the car. The Court thought it appropriate for you to come to the hospital two years ago and now we will reassess the situation. That is going to require a certain amount of time."

Illanna withdrew into herself, trying to mentally prepare for the ordeal ahead.

III

Johnson accompanied Illanna and the matron to the Admissions Office and then returned to the Administration Building. Fortunado was waiting in his outer office.

"What happened?"

"Let's go inside."

Johnson led Dick into his office.

"They arrested John."

Fortunado swept this aside impatiently. "I knew that. What happened with the girl?"

"She was the one."

"I knew it. John got her out and has been shacking up with her all this time."

Johnson looked disgustedly at the Director. Fortunado seemed to be relishing all of this. "We don't know if John had anything to do with her escape, or what their relationship is, and frankly, it's really none of our business. John has enough problems with the murders hanging over his head . . . he doesn't need allegations about events that took place two years ago."

"But it might tie into his motive. If Azahdi and Goldstein had found out about his helping her to escape, that could explain the whole thing."

"Maybe." Johnson shook his head doubtfully. "In any event, it's out of our hands now. We don't have to do Schneider's work for him. Ms. Romanowsky is another matter. We do have to deal with her."

Fortunado was looking out of the window and Johnson couldn't see the crafty look which came into his eyes. He turned to Johnson. "What are you going to do about her?"

"She will have to be reevaluated, and we will have to check with the Court on how they want to proceed."

"What ward are you going to send her to?"

"The Admissions Ward, I suppose."

"Isn't that the ward where there was a question about the aide?"

"Yes."

"Is the aide still up there?"

"I don't know. I forgot his name."

"Franklin." Fortunado's reply was instantaneous.

Johnson looked at him sharply. "How do you remember that name after two years?"

"Oh. You remember you asked me to check into it at the time?" Fortunado was too casual.

Johnson's level of suspicion should have been raised, but he was too concerned about John and the disposition of Illanna's case. "We better find out if he's still on the ward."

It seemed as though Fortunado was going to speak again, but he checked himself. Johnson called Nursing Administration. "Is there an aide named Franklin working on the Admission Ward? . . . I see." He hung up the phone. "He's still up there."

"We'd better not send her up there, then. We don't need union trouble on top of everything else."

"No. But where can she go?"

"There are only four locked wards in the hospital," Fortunado responded, "the Admission Ward, the violent ward in the Psychiatric Treatment Center, the regressed ward in the Long Term Care Center, and the regressed ward in Geriatrics."

"Not too many good choices."

"Only one as far as I can see," said Fortunado.

"Which do you think is best?"

"Well, we have eliminated the Admission Ward, but she has to be on a locked ward until the Court has made its determination. The Geriatrics Ward is inappropriate, and she would hardly survive on the Violent Ward, so that leaves the locked ward in Long Term Care."

"Can they do all of the admission workup over there?"

"They will bitch about it, but they have the personnel. I'll supervise it personally."

"Okay. I guess we don't have a choice. I'll set it up with the Admissions Office. She's over there now."

Something was nagging at the back of Johnson's mind, but he was too relieved at having resolved the problem, at least temporarily, to try to figure out what it was.

Fortunado got back to his office in a hurry, and phoned Rachel. "We've got her."

"Johnson bought it?"

"There really wasn't anything else he could do, but we are going to have to work fast. The Court may let her go."

"How much time do we have?"

"They won't be able to get a hearing for at least a week."

"That should be enough time."

"It's going to have to be. And Rachel, be careful. This could blow up in our faces."

"Don't worry. I know what I'm doing."

"Okay. I'll bring her over after she's admitted."

Fortunado hoped Rachel was as competent as she was confident. He was up and pacing, thinking about the many possibilities and everything that could go wrong.

Illanna went through the admission procedure in a daze. The same questions. The same old lady across the desk as two years ago. Thought of escaping flickered through her mind. The charge nurse from the admission ward was between her and the only exit. Worry for John, fear for herself, confusion tumbled through her mind. She answered the questions mechanically.

"Illanna Romanowsky. Twenty-five. No residence."

"No residence?"

"Didn't they tell you? I live on the wind."

"This will go a lot faster if you cooperate, young lady."

"I'm not in a hurry."

The elderly woman sighed and went on to the next line. After the forms were completed, the Admission Officer called over to Administration, and Fortunado came over personally to escort Illanna to Extended Care. He wanted a chance to talk to her alone. They began the half-mile walk to Extended Care.

"You have created a lot of problems for the Hospital."

"Don't you mean that I have created problems for you and Rachel?"

"Spreading lies about us and trying to implicate us in the murders is what got you back here. If you continue, things could get worse for you."

"I don't see how. They've got John locked up for something you did and me for something I'm not."

"Believe me, your stay here can be easy or hard. It depends on your attitude."

"I'm not going to be here long."

"We'll see."

Fortunado half-wanted her to try to escape. More evidence of her instability and the necessity for tight controls. Illanna knew her limits. She was no match for the Director physically, and anyway, how far would she get on foot with security cars patrolling and guards at the gates?

They arrived at the Long Term Care Building, and Fortunado ushered her past the nursing station into Rachel's office. Rachel stood up behind her desk and walked around to meet her.

"So this is Illanna. John has told us so little about you."

The two stood toe to toe, each appraising the other. Rachel was twenty years older than Illanna but still clung to her youthful beauty. She was dark like the Gypsy, her hair short and straight. Illanna's ringlets gave way to jet tresses hanging long down her back. Rachel was below medium height and stocky, Illanna taller and willowy. Both had dark eyes which seemed to spark as they held the other's glance.

"We haven't formally met. I'm Rachel Slade."

"I know."

"We are going to try to help you."

"Do what?"

"Why . . . get better of course."

Illanna laughed. It was not a pretty sound.

Fortunado interposed, "I told her things would be much better for her if she cooperated."

"He's right, you know." Rachel said it kindly, but there was steel in her voice.

"I'm really a problem for the two of you, aren't I? I know what you are and what you have done. You have to discredit me and John, but you can't harm me."

"Harm you? My dear, we only want to help you." Rachel was purring like a cat who has her paw resting on a mouse. "Now, let's get you settled."

She rang for an orderly who took Illanna up to the locked ward. When she had gone, Rachel closed the door and turned to Fortunado.

"We are going to have to kill her."

Dick was startled by her bluntness. "We didn't have to kill Randy, and she doesn't know as much as he does."

"Don't confuse this one with the patients. She's smart and dangerous and not any crazier than you and me."

"But what can she do to us? No one will believe her. They will just think it's delusional talk."

"Not if she and John are telling the same story about what they saw up at the cabin and not if the Court lets her go next week . . . which it will."

"It's too dangerous. She's in our keeping now . . .   If anything happens . . ." Fortunado trailed off.

"Leave it to me. They won't even know what happened to her . . . She's run off before."

Fortunado wasn't convinced but left for the Administration Building with Rachel's promise that she wouldn't do anything until they worked everything out. They still had a week.

The Long Term Care Building was the newest building on the grounds. It was almost like a college dormitory except for the locked doors and the security screens on the windows. Illanna had a single room and was permitted to keep her own clothing. She might even have relaxed a little except for an incident which occurred on the way up.

The elevators were located in the center of the building with the locked male and female wards off to either side of a central day room on the second floor. As Illanna and the aide stepped off the elevator, Illanna almost cried out because Randy was sitting on one of the couches neat the elevator. She quickly suppressed the cry, however, when she saw his fixed stare and zombie-like posture. She passed within two feet and there was no flicker of recognition.

"What did they do to him?"

"You know him? He's zonked on Thorazine."

"Why?"

"He tore up the ward over the weekend."

"He was all right on Saturday."

The aide looked at her with curiosity. "How do you know that?"

"He was out on pass with Dr. Lowell at the Eastern Championship Weight Lifting Meet."

"So that's it."

"What do you mean?"

"He went off the deep end when he got back."

"Why?"

"They said because Dr. Lowell had him off medications for the meet."

"But John . . . Dr. Lowell said he got permission to take him off medications months ago."

"Yeah . . . I guess so. But he was really wild Saturday night."

"Do you know what happened?"

"I wasn't on duty, but I read the progress notes on it. It started with an argument with the charge nurse on third shift. She called a male aide and Randy got into a fight with him. It wasn't much of a fight. Randy hit him once, knocked him against a wall and he's down at the General Hospital with multiple fractures."

"But what started it? Randy was really on a high when we got him back. He had just won the heavyweight power lifting championship."

"There was something in the notes about a trophy. The nurse was trying to confiscate it."

"Oh, my God! No wonder Randy got upset."
Illanna pondered over what had happened to
Randy, but couldn't dwell on it for long
because of her own problems and John's
situation. She had to sort everything out and
devise some sort of plan.

The machinery of the hospital ground
inexorably on. She had physicals,
psychologicals, social service interviews . . .
the same questions over and over again. Her
initial team meeting was scheduled for
Tuesday morning.

IV

They sat around the table, each trying to look a little more bored than the next. It was unusual for the Director to sit in on the Team meeting, and they thought boredom was professional. The psychiatrist was at the head of the table, presiding over the motley group. He looked through his reading glasses vaguely at the assessment information from all the disciplines. The caseworker kept brushing the hair back from her unprepossessing face. The psychologist stared at the ash tray as if he expected it to levitate. The nurse scrooched down in her chair and kept darting looks at Rachel out of the corner of her eye.

"I'm sitting in on Team today because this is an unusual case, and I have special knowledge about this woman's background which I think the Team should be aware of ."

The psychiatrist took the lead. "Ahem. Well, you are certainly welcome, Rachel. It's always nice to have another pretty face at the table. Ha, ha."

"Thank you," Rachel purred. "Much of what I say must remain off the record," the ward clerk stopped writing abruptly, "because there are staff members involved, and there will be a court proceeding next week, so that Ms. Romanowsky's chart will almost certainly be subpoenaed."

The psychiatrist lost his bored look and squirmed uncomfortably in his chair. He didn't like court proceedings. Those damn lawyers and their questions.

"Ms. Romanowsky is a former patient at the Hospital." Eyebrows were raised around the table. "You wouldn't remember her. She was here for a day two years ago. You probably heard of the incident. She escaped, and at the time we thought she had inside help, but we didn't know who was involved. It appears now that Dr. Lowell was the one who got her out."

There were gasps and whistles around the table. Rachel had them in the palm of her hand. She continued. "As you know, Dr. Lowell has been arrested in connection with the deaths of Dr. Azahdi and Senator Goldstein. There may be a connection between their deaths and Ms. Romanowsky's escape. Apparently, Azahdi found out something and was in communication with Goldstein shortly before they were murdered. It may have been Lowell's involvement with Illanna."

The caseworker interrupted, "How arc we supposed to handle this case?"

Rachel smiled. "I am not going to presume to tell the Team how to handle the case, but I wanted to give you some background so that

you won't be in the dark when you interview
Ms. Romanowsky this morning. She is a very
clever and dangerous woman, if you want my
opinion."

"Go on," urged the psychiatrist.

"Illanna appears to be a highly intelligent
paranoid. I don't know how she conned
John, but I can guess."

The caseworker tittered.

"Anyway, she claims to be a witch. She is now
saying that I am also a witch and that Dr.
Fortunado and I are the ones responsible for
Azahdi's and Goldstein's deaths."

"Ridiculous," the psychiatrist snorted.

"Don't be too hard on her, remember she's
crazy." Rachel oozed compassion.

"How should we handle the interview?"

"Be careful not to get pulled into a discussion
of the murders. Remember she is due to go
back to court shortly and John's arraignment
is also coming up. Anything said in her
presence may get into one or both of those
proceedings. I don't care about myself, but
you all don't want to get dragged into this
business."

The psychiatrist cleared his throat, "I'll
handle the interview. The rest of you follow
my lead."

Rachel pulled her chair back into the shadows of the corner of the room, and the nurse went to get Illanna.

Illanna blinked, coming from the garishly lit hallway into the dimly lit room. She looked at the rogues' gallery around the table, but her attention quickly became riveted on the shadowy figure in the corner. She could feel rather than fully see the force of Rachel's presence in the room. The nurse led her to an empty seat across the corner of the table from the Psychiatrist. Her back was to the corner of the room where Rachel sat.

"Good morning . . . Ms. Romanowsky, is it? How are you today?"

"I've been better."

"Ahem. Yes, of course. This is a Team Meeting. I believe you have met everyone here."

Illanna threw her head back toward the corner where Rachel sat. "Is she in on this?"

"mm . . . . That is the Director of the Unit, Mrs. Rachel Slade. She is not a regular member of the Team."

"That's a relief."

"Now, now, Ms. Romanowsky. Belligerence will not help your cause."

"Which is?"

"I beg your pardon?"

"Which cause are we talking about?"

"Why, your getting better of course."

"Better at what?"

"Uh . . . getting out of the Hospital."

"Now, there's a cause I can believe in. Are you all going to get me out?" Illanna looked intently at each member of the Team. They squirmed sequentially as her piercing look swept around the table.

"That is certainly our goal, but first we have to resolve some of the little problems that got you in here."

"The little problem that got me in here was a two hundred and fifty pound matron from the County Jail. I don't believe any two of you could resolve her."

"Ha, ha. It's healthy to have a sense of humor."

"Ha, ha. It's not hard to have a sense of humor around here. Look at you. Miss Social Work over there looking like a fugitive from an acne commercial, the Psychologist trying to look at one eye with the other, Nursey has to keep propping herself up so her head doesn't slide down into that neat starched uniform and you . . . do you sew those Princeton

University Shop labels in yourself, or does a
maid come in?"

"Really, Ms. Romanowsky, we don't have to sit
here and listen to that kind of personal
abuse."

"That's true enough. You are all dismissed."
Illanna waved her hand.

"Ms. Romanowsky will have her little joke."
The voice was like ice. All heads turned
toward the darkened corner except Illanna's.
She stared straight ahead. "I really advise you
to cooperate, Illanna. So far everyone has
tried to make things pleasant for you, but you
are making that very difficult."

Illanna didn't reply. The psychiatrist turned
back toward her. "Yes, of course we know
you are under a strain."

"Let's cut the bullshit. I don't know what she's
been telling you about me, and personally I
don't care. My hearing has to be within five
days of admission. I'm not going to give you
any ammunition to keep me here. I've
answered all of your silly questions about my
mother and father and when I stopped wetting
the bed. So let's just wait for the hearing, and
then I'll say what I have to say.."

"But what are we supposed to put down on
your treatment plan?"

"Put down I don't plan on being treated by any of you, and if you can all contain yourselves for a couple of days, I'll be out of here."

Rachel spoke again. "There's really no point in going on with this. Will you escort Ms. Romanowsky back to her room?"

The nurse led Illanna out. The Team sat in stunned silence. The psychologist was the first to speak. "Well! In all my years at the Hospital, I have never been talked to by a patient in such a fashion!"

Rachel almost said something which would hardly have been complimentary to the PhD. She had developed a grudging respect for Illanna during the interview, but it wasn't in her interest to let the Team see it. "Let's keep in mind that she is not a well woman."

"Oh . . . of course." The psychologist regained his smug, superior smile. "I'm sure she will be in a better humor in a couple of days and we can schedule her again."

The Team filed out, but Rachel motioned the psychiatrist to stay. "You can see what we are up against, Doctor. She has a tongue like a knife. There is no telling what she might say in Court."

"Yes . . . but what can we do?"

"She is obviously disturbed and delusional. What do you usually do with disturbed and delusional patients?"

"But she won't consent to taking medications."

"You know she doesn't have to. Not in the State on an involuntary commitment. You give the order, and I'll see she gets the treatment."

The psychiatrist shook his head dubiously. "I don't know . . . I usually like to observe the patient for awhile . . ."

"Okay, suit yourself. If you don't mind her running around the ward making fools of . . ."

 "Oh, all right, what do you want me to do?"

Rachel outlined her medication regimen quickly and then led the psychiatrist down the hall to sign the orders. In her office she called Fortunado.

"She played right into our hands . . . That's right. She made idiots of them. You have to admire her, but I told you, she's dangerous. She says she is going to say her piece in court . . . Never mind, I took care of it . . . No, of course not . . . Not yet. In a few minutes she is going to be so zonked out she won't know who *she* is, much less who we are and what we've done . . . No, the drugs won't work in Court. That Civil liberties-type will ask first thing what medication she is on and how

much. We can't risk it . . . I know we can't,
but she has escaped before. Who says she
won't again? . . . Not where she's going."

Rachel hung up the phone and gazed out the
window, her eyes slits against the light.

Illanna heard them coming down the hall.
She was ready. She jumped in bed and
turned toward the wall. She didn't move when
she felt her pajama bottoms tugged down and
hardly flinched at the sting of the needle.

V

"Sh! Wake up, Randy."

"Uh! . . . Whatsa matter?"

Rachel shook the massive shoulder in the darkened room. "We have a job to do."

"What?"

"Never mind, get up."

Rachel propped him up and helped him pull on his coveralls. She peeked out the door. The dorm was quiet. The dim night lights barely lit the long hallway. She led Randy stumbling along to the fire exit and around to the women's side. The third shift staff were having coffee in the nursing station and weren't due to make rounds for another fifteen minutes. They entered Illanna's room at the end of the hall.

"Pick her up."

"Who?"

"Pick her up, Randy, and follow me."

Randy picked up the huddled form and threw it over his shoulder as easily as if it had been a rag doll. Rachel led the way to the other fire exit and down the steps to the basement. Randy rolled along behind her, grabbing the railing with his free hand to keep from falling. He had a glazed look in his eyes, which was only partially due to being awakened in the middle of the night.

Behind the linen rack at the end of the laundry room was an old door.

Rachel inserted a skeleton key and swung the linen rack and door open far enough for Randy to sidle through with his burden. She locked the door silently behind her. The tunnel was pitch black. She switched on her flashlight and started down the long corridor. The shadows on the wall took on fantastic shapes as the misshapen hulk lumbered along after the black robed figure. After 100 yards, another door opened out on the main tunnel between Geriatrics and the Administration Building. Rachel looked up and down the partially lighted tunnel. Lights streaked off into the gloom in both directions with no sign of life. She started across the main tunnel and stopped dead. She thought she heard a faint echo of footsteps far off toward the Geriatrics Building. She could see nothing, so she crossed the main tunnel quickly and pressed hard on a brick halfway up the wall. The brick pivoted, revealing a keyhole. Rachel inserted another skeleton key and pushed on the wall. A four foot section pivoted, revealing another tunnel. She hustled Randy with his burden through the opening and locked it behind them.

The danger was passed. No one beside her and Fortunado, and now Randy, knew the secret entrance to the crypt beneath the morgue. Some craftsmen in the early days of the century had walled the entrances off and, for reasons which would probably never be known, had made them accessible by the two secret doors. The tunnels were never reopened, and their existence had been forgotten until Fortunado had come across some old blueprints of the Hospital. The side tunnel began to slope down toward the morgue. Rachel opened the iron gate at the end and ushered Randy into the stone vault. Fortunado was already there in his full Devil's robes.

"Why didn't you blindfold him?"

"There wasn't time, and he's so far under he won't remember any of this anyway."

"What are we going to do?"

"I've always wanted to do a human sacrifice."

"But the body?"

"The room behind the sarcophagus has stone coffins. They will never find this place, and even if they do, we can get rid of the body before that."

Fortunado's thin lips twitched beneath the mask. "Then let's get on with it."

Rachel stripped Illanna and lay her naked body on the stone alter. Fortunado took a step toward her.

"Get back. She's not for you."

He moved back outside the pentagram, muttering to himself. Randy rocked back and forth, spittle drooling out of the side of his mouth. He began to moan.

"Quiet," Rachel hissed.

She fastened leather straps to Illanna's ankles and wrists and lit candles at the points of the Devil's star.

Rachel began the ancient chant. Her cadence became faster and faster and her voice more strident. The figure on the alter moved slightly, and Illanna's eyes began to flutter. She saw the black-robed figure swaying above her, ceremonial knife glinting in the candle light, and screamed.

CHAPTER NINE -- SUGAR BEAR

I

The room was sterile white, even the bed. John's eyes fluttered and then opened slowly. He was completely disoriented. Gradually, the events of the last few days came flooding back. He still couldn't figure out where he was. This should be the jail. His right arm was restricted.

He glanced over at it and saw that his wrist was handcuffed to the post at the head of the bed. The movement stirred a figure sitting by the window. It was Schneider. He came over to the bed, a relieved look on his face.

"So, you're awake?"

"Getting there. Where am I? What happened?"

"You attacked a guard and I had to clip you with my revolver. I'm afraid I hit you harder than I meant to."

"Illanna?"

"She's all right. Back at the hospital."

John jerked half upright, but the handcuffs pulled him back. "She can't go back there! She . . ."

"She's all right, John! Her hearing will be in a couple of days, and I'm sure they will let her loose."

"What about Rachel and Fortunado?"

"What about them?"

"Do you think they are going to sit back and do nothing with Illanna and me knowing what we do about them?"

"What do you know about them?"

"I know they are involved in some kind of devil cult at the Hospital."

"Your only evidence is what you heard from Randy. Even you must admit that he is not a very reliable witness."

"Randy wouldn't lie to me, or Illanna either for that matter."

"Perhaps not, but does *he* know the truth? How much in contact with reality is he?"

"Randy's not delusional, if that's what you mean."

"I don't think his testimony would be acceptable in a court of law."

"We're not talking about a court of law. We're talking about Illanna's safety."

"Be reasonable, John. Even if what you suspect is true, they wouldn't dare do anything at the Hospital. Not with us suspecting them."

"Then you do suspect them."

"Well, appearance to the contrary, I still don't think you and Illanna are involved."

John relaxed a little. "What are you going to do?"

"Now that I don't have to worry about you two for awhile . . . continue the investigation."

"Will they let you?"

"Let me? They will insist on it. The chief thinks you're it, but he still needs more evidence."

"Against me?"

"That's what he wants, but it doesn't mean that's what I'll find."

"I'm still worried about Illanna. She doesn't belong there, and she will be worried about me."

"I'm going up this afternoon. I'll check on her."

"Thanks."

The infirmary nurse came in, and Schneider left, promising to return later with a report on

Illanna. John absently cooperated as the prison nurse went through her bedside routine, but his mind was still in a turmoil. Kaleidoscopic images of Rachel dancing around the fire, dogs leaping at him and Illanna's terror-stricken face kept flashing through his throbbing head. He couldn't think. He drifted off into a troubled sleep.

II

Schneider drove slowly to the Hospital. He had a two o'clock appointment with Johnson. The terrors of the Hospital were mostly gone now. Judy was a positive attraction, and he didn't fear meeting his mother nearly as much as he had. John had done that. The bulldog in Schneider was beginning to assert itself. He was convinced of John's innocence, and however irrational that might be, it meant that he had to ferret out the real Malleus. Fortunado was a possibility, but he wasn't counting on it. He had the layman's prejudice against the reliability of mental patients. Clinicians who are around psychosis all of the time notice that in the most psychotic patient there are pockets of sanity. Within these pockets, the patient is as rational as anyone else. Very rarely are delusional systems all-encompassing, and in many forms of mental illness delusions are not present at all.

The criminal justice system in the United States, in bending over backward to protect the rights of the accused, is always skeptical about the reliability of testimony. It doesn't take much of a lawyer to destroy the credibility of a witness with a history of mental illness. All the lawyer has to do is probe until he brings out the irrational part of the patient's thinking. Everyone is irrational to a degree when the ego structure is threatened. The irrationality is more visible and dramatic in a psychotic patient. John was convinced not only of the truthfulness of Randy's statements but the accuracy as far as they went. Schneider was willing to dismiss it all as the thinking of a crazy person. John's and Illanna's experience up at the cabin was another matter.

Johnson was staring out of the window when Schneider came into his office. He turned, startled, and seemed not to recognize Schneider for a moment.

"Am I interrupting?"

"No . . . No. Come on in."

"You seem preoccupied."

"Oh . . . Yes. This business of John and Ms. Romanowsky . . . very upsetting."

"That's what I came to talk to you about."

"Yes?"

"John is very concerned about Illanna."

Johnson stiffened. "We are all concerned about her. It is the nature of our business to be concerned with all of our patients."

"Of course. There is no implication . . ."

"I'm sorry. I shouldn't be so touchy. But you see the gravity of all of this. Murders occurring within the Hospital. Now the possibility of staff involvement. A possible sexual relationship between a staff member and patient. The public is rarely charitable about what goes on in a State Hospital. This is turning into the biggest scandal ever, and we've been here a long time. And with all of that, I still don't think John is guilty."

"That's really what I want to talk to you about."

"You don't think John is guilty either?"

"No."

"But you had him arrested."

"Under orders from my supervisors. We are getting a lot of heat too."

"What are you going to do?"

"Continue the investigation with an open mind."

"How can I help?"

"Well, first of all, I would like to get the business cleared up about Dr. Fortunado and Rachel Slade."

Johnson frowned. "That's a bunch of nonsense."

"Which part?"

"What do you mean?"

"Well, according to John, Randy claims there is some sort of devil cult in the Hospital that Rachel Slade is involved with. John claims that he and Illanna witnessed a ceremony with Rachel and Fortunado up at his cabin on Sunday. I am willing to dismiss the testimony of Randy, but it's not so straight-forward with John's statement."

"On the contrary. I see it quite in reverse."

"The reverse?"

"I assigned John the task of finding Malleus among our residents. He has been searching the files for evidence of a patient's delusional system which revolved around witches, the devil, etc. He may have come across it in his dealing with Randy."

"And?"

"Even if John is not himself guilty, he has a very close relationship with Randy. In order to protect Randy and himself. he has to place the guilt elsewhere."

"You think he would do that?"

"If he is guilty he would certainly do that."

"And if he is innocent?"

"He might do it anyway to protect Randy and give himself the freedom to look further."

Schneider scratched his head. "Well, that's certainly an alternative possibility. I would still like to talk to Mrs. Slade and Dr. Fortunado, however."

"That's easily arranged with Dick. He's right down the hall.

Johnson pushed the intercom button. "Dick, are you busy?"

A disembodied voice came back. "No more than usual."

"Detective Schneider is here and would like to speak with you."

"Send him down."

Johnson directed Schneider to the end of the hall, and he was ushered into Fortunado's office by the Social Service Secretary. Fortunado didn't rise but looked directly at the detective. There was considerable hostility in the gaze. Schneider in turn held the eyes in a way that the Director was not used to. It was like the confrontation between a mongoose and a cobra. The adversaries were evenly matched.

Fortunado made the first move. "How is John?"

"John is fine . . . considering the circumstances. I need some information from you."

"How can I help?" Somehow Fortunado's tone did not suggest he wanted to be particularly helpful.

"I'll be direct, if I may. John claims that you and Rachel Slade are involved in a devil's cult at the Hospital."

Fortunado did not respond immediately. When he did, it was with a venomously controlled voice. "And on what does he base such a ridiculous accusation?"

"Two things. Randy Stoltzfoos's testimony that he and other patients are involved in devil worship here at the Hospital . . ."

"Pardon me. Did Randy say I was involved?"

"Well . . . no. He claims Mrs. Slade and someone else . . ."

"But not me in particular?"

"No."

"And the second thing?"

"Dr. Lowell claims that he and Illanna saw you and Mrs. Slade involved in a ritual of some sort up at your cabin."

"It seems to me the testimony of a mental patient on the one hand and an accused murderer on the other is somewhat less than convincing."

"I'm not suggesting that I am convinced, but I would like to hear your side of the story."

"When did I stop beating my wife? No, Lieutenant, I am not going to dignify the accusation with an explanation. There is no basis in any of it. It should be clear to you John's motive in making the whole thing up."

"Then you deny it?"

"Certainly."

"Do you mind telling me where you were when Dr. Azahdi and Senator Goldstein were murdered?"

Fortunado did not over-play his hand by asking when that was.

He flipped through the appointment calendar on his desk.

"I had no appointments the morning Dr. Azahdi was killed. There are no notations, so I was probably in my office or in the building all morning. I really don't remember. When Senator Goldstein was killed I was at the teaching conference, along with at least 100 staff and assorted patients."

"Where were you sitting?"

"Toward the back of the chapel."

"And on Sunday?"

"I was up at my cabin."

"With Mrs. Slade?"

"That's really none of your business, but yes, Rachel was up there on Sunday."

"What were you doing?"

"Really, Schneider, this is insufferable. I have Sundays off. What I do on my own property with my friends is not police business."

"I'm sorry. I must pursue this. John's accusations have to be dealt with."

"My relationship with Mrs. Slade is personal. We are not involved in any devil cult and that is all there is to that."

Schneider saw he was getting nowhere and excused himself.

Security called the Long Term Care Center and arranged for him to meet with Mrs. Slade.

Rachel had already talked to Fortunado on the phone before Schneider was out of the Administration Building. "Come in, Lieutenant."

Schneider had formed some opinions about Mrs. Slade from hearing about her from John and various members of the staff. He was not disappointed in meeting her in person. Many people look like what they do in the work setting. That is, their personal idiosyncrasies are submerged in the function they perform. With Rachel it was the reverse.

She looked nothing like a nurse who had risen by dint of hard work to an administrative position. Rather she looked like an attractive intelligent woman who could be anything she wanted and happened to be the administrator of this unit. Her surroundings were an expansion of herself. The office was tastefully decorated, just being saved from looking like a living room by the presence of her desk. Unlike Fortunado, she met Schneider half-way and motioned for him to sit on a couch while she sat in an easy chair across from him. "How can I help you?"

The voice was sugar-coated compared to the venomous response of the Social Service Director, but Schneider did not get the feeling that she wanted to be helpful either. "A couple of things. First, Dr. Lowell wanted me to see how Miss Romanowsky was doing."

"I'm afraid John's interest in Illanna has lost some of its professional distance . . . If there ever was any."

"Nevertheless, I am also interested in her progress."

"She is currently undergoing evaluations by all of the various disciplines in preparation for her hearing."

"Which is when?"

"The Court has not set a time at present, but according to the usual practice, it has to be within five days of admission which would be within four days from now . . . certainly by the end of the week."

"Where is she now?"

"On our unit."

"Why?"

"What do you mean?"

"Isn't it customary for new admissions to go to the admissions ward?"

"Yes."

"Then why the change in the procedure?"

"It was at the request of the Superintendent."

"Really?"

"You can check with him."

"What was his reason?"

"I'm not sure I am at liberty to go into that. It involves clinical matters and confidential personnel information."

"I can find out."

"Not from me." Some of the sugar had gone out of Rachel's voice and her lustrous brown eyes were going to flint.

"But is she all right?"

"Depends on how you look at it. Physically she is fine."

"But mentally?"

"It's hard for me to be objective. She is making wild accusations about me which I know to be untrue. Either she is delusional . . . crazy . . . or trying to save John and herself from this mess."

"Which?"

"That's up to the psychiatrist to determine."

"May I speak to him?"

"I doubt if he will tell you anything before her commitment hearing."

"I can get a court order."

"I doubt if you can arrange that before the hearing, but you are welcome to try."

"Her accusations bring me to the second reason I wanted to see you."

"Yes?"

"I'm sorry if I have to be direct, but I would like your version of what went on up at Dr. Fortunado's cabin on Sunday."

Schneider could tell by her acceptance of the question that she had been in touch with the Social Service Director. This was not in and of itself an admission of guilt, but it added to Bob's suspicion that the two were hiding something.

"You have talked to Dick?"

"Yes, but he wasn't very helpful."

"I shouldn't wonder."

"Yes?"

"I imagine he resents the invasion of his privacy as much as I do."

"I appreciate that, but this is a criminal matter and we have to know certain things."

"What criminal matter? Was a crime committed on Sunday?"

"No . . . but . . ."

"No buts. I can account for my time when the crimes were committed, and I imagine Dick can also. I was at his cabin on Sunday . . . not that it is any of your business, and what we did there is certainly not."

"Okay. Where were you when Azahdi and Goldstein were killed?"

"I had a conference with two of the aides from this building at the time when Azahdi was supposedly killed, and I was at the teaching conference, along with half of the staff at the hospital, when Goldstein was killed."

"Where were you sitting?"

"Toward the back."

"With Fortunado."

"Dr. Fortunado . . . Yes."

"And neither of you left your seats during the entire conference?"

"No."

Schneider noted the information in his book. "Now may I please see Ms. Romanowsky?"

"No."

Schneider was taken aback. "Why not?"

"I told you she is being evaluated . . . going through a number of tests."

"But surely she has a few minutes . . ."

"Her schedule is beside the point. We do not want her disturbed during this period."

"I don't think it will disturb her to hear how John is doing."

"We will be the judge of that."

"I'm afraid I must insist on seeing her."

"Not without a court injunction."

Schneider glared at Rachel. He was unused to this kind of obstruction and he was beginning to understand some of John's fears. These people had as much control over the patients as the criminal justice system had over prisoners. "Mrs. Slade, I find your attitude highly suspicious."

"My 'attitude' as you call it is directed toward the well-being of a patient and I will not permit her to be disturbed by police questioning at this time."

"I may be back."

"Any time . . . with a court injunction."

Schneider walked out of Rachel's office completely frustrated. There was certainly not much he could tell John, and there was little he knew about Fortunado and Mrs. Slade that he hadn't known going in. Two suggestive trends had emerged, however. One was the close communication between Fortunado and Rachel. He had obviously called her immediately after the interview . . . to get their stories straight? Probably. And the refusal to let him see Illanna was suspicious and a little ominous. He was not nearly as sure of her safety now as he had been when he talked to John. He decided to go over to Geriatrics and talk to Judy.

As he crossed between the two buildings he saw a familiar figure sitting on a bench.

"Hello, Sonny."

"Hello, Mother." It came out so naturally that Schneider was halfway to the bench before he realized the admission of the greeting. His mother didn't seem to notice, but took it in her stride.

"I was expecting you."

"I know."

Schneider sat down beside the frail woman. He looked at her with new eyes. The fear was gone. The emotions playing within him were ambivalent but mostly pleasant. Curiosity, compassion . . . love? He didn't know. He remembered her as a young woman with long black hair. She was still beautiful in a wan, transparent sort of way. Her hair was short and absolutely white. She was looking at him with curiosity also. People did not go along so readily with her fantasy, and she frequently knew it was a fantasy. Hadn't she seen this young man before?

"Are you going to take me home?"

"Maybe. I have to talk to your doctor and the rest of the Team."

The tears welled up in the old lady's eyes. "I know I'm a crazy old lady, but please don't lie to me. You're not really my son."

"I am, Mother."

"Oh God!" She put her hands over her face and wept. Schneider put his arm around her shoulder.

"It's all right, Mother. We will work it out."

She leaned against him, and the sobbing slowly subsided. "I've been waiting such a long time."

"I know, but you don't have to wait any longer. I will come and visit you as often as I can, and we will work on getting you out of here. Now I have to go over to the Geriatrics Ward. I'll stop in and see you tomorrow."

Schneider leaned over and kissed her on the cheek. She watched him all the way as he climbed the long hill to the Geriatrics Building. Judy smiled as he walked in.

"Hello."

A relieved look came over Schneider's face. "You're not angry with me?"

"For what?"

"Arresting John."

"Wasn't it your duty?"

"Yes."

"I know about duty." She smiled. "It was hard for you, wasn't it?"

"Very hard . . . still is."

"How is John?"

"He's okay. I had to clip him behind the ear downtown, but he seems none the worse for wear."

"You had to hit him?"

Schneider explained the situation as it had developed in the visiting room. Judy's mouth dropped open when she heard about Illanna and remained that way as revelation after revelation came tumbling out of the detective.

"My God! John is really in trouble. Even if he can get himself out from under this murder business, his career is over."

"Why?"

"There are certain things which are taboo within the State Mental Health System. The first taboo is that of sexual involvement with patients."

"But Illanna isn't really a patient . . . certainly wasn't when she became involved with John."

"Technically, she has been a patient since she was admitted two years ago. John's behavior certainly has not been professional."

"That's true, but it has been understandable."

"This is not an understanding system."

"Well, in any event, we have more immediate problems. We've got to clear John of the murders and get Illanna out of here."

Judy almost laughed.

"What are you grinning about?"

"Do you know how much you have changed in the last week?"

Schneider thought back over the recent events. "A lot has happened."

"A lot has happened inside of you."

"Like what?"

"Well, John would say you have become a *mensch.*"

Schneider was offended.

"I wasn't a human being before?"

"Don't pout. You were a machine. Nothing mattered but the law. When I first met you, I thought immediately of Javert in <u>Les</u>

Miserables. Do you know what your nickname was after your first day here?"

"No . . . what?"

"Weasel."

"That's not very complimentary."

"No . . . but it was fairly accurate."

"That's not . . ."

"Don't get upset. I said it was accurate. Now you're a pussy cat."

Schneider laughed. "The pussy cat still has claws."

"Meow," Judy flirted.

"I'll be over this counter in a second."

"Wait till tonight."

They laughed and talked as young lovers for a while, forgetting about the problems of the last several days . . . caught up with each other and the renewal of life which love can bring.

"I saw my mother again on my way over here."

A look of apprehension spread over Judy's face. "Oh?" she said cautiously.

"I told her who I was."

"Oh, Bob! That's wonderful. What did she say?"

"I think she understood and believed me. I don't know if she will remember, though."

"I'm sure she will."

"There is so much I don't understand about this schizophrenic business. I've read so much, but until I talked to her it all seemed so unreal, clinical . . . I don't know."

"It's because you see her as a person, as your mother and not as a schizophrenic. So, aside from wanting to jump my bones in the nursing station, why did you come over?"

"Isn't that enough of a reason?"

"Yes . . . but I know you. You either combine business with pleasure, or business with business. So what's the business?"

"Well, you know Illanna is back in the hospital and over in the Long Term Care Center."

"You said."

"I was interviewing Rachel."

Judy's brown eyes darkened. "Mrs. Slade?"

"Yes."

"And?"

"She refused to let me talk to Illanna. What I want to know is the hospital's policy generally."

Judy paused a moment before responding. "The relationship between our patients and the police is often quite complicated. Many of our patients have some involvement with the law before they come in. In fact, the majority of the patients have at least bent the law by their behavior in the community, and that is why they are in here. The hospital tries to protect the legal rights of the patients, but our policies are dictated more by what is clinically best for the patient. In Illanna's case, I can't see any clinical reason why you should not be allowed to see her."

"There is no legal reason either. It's in our interest to have her out of here so we can deal with her directly."

"What did Slade give as *her* reason for not allowing you to see Illanna?"

"She said it was not their policy to allow interviews while the assessment procedure was going on."

"Well, I can tell you for a fact that is a bunch of bullshit."

"Why?"

"Because they do not *have* a policy. I bet they don't get two direct admissions a year over there. That is always handled by the Admission Unit."

"Then what *is* her reason for not letting me see her?"

"I don't know."

"It's got me worried. John believes that she and Fortunado may do something to keep her from talking. I think it's ridiculous. What can they do to her in here with all of the safeguards you have in place?"

Judy looked at him pityingly. "You really are naïve. We have much more control over patients here than you do in prison. We can medicate them without their consent, for one thing."

"Yes, but Rachel doesn't control the medical regimen."

"You don't know Slade. She has every psychiatrist in the Unit intimidated or sexually in her pocket."

"Oh . . .come on!"

"I'm not just being catty."

Bob looked at Judy, his eyebrows cocked quizzically.

"Well . . . maybe a little catty, but it is well known that she controls everything in her Unit one way or another."

"I'm hoping she is just buying time for her and Fortunado to get their act together before Illanna gets out of here and starts telling her story."

"Then you believe John and Illanna?"

"As far as it goes. It's fairly bizarre, what he describes that took place at Fortunado's. I can pretty well verify it if I can talk to Illanna independently of John."

"How?"

"Give me some credit for being good at my job."

"Of course."

"If people stick to a very simple description of events, then two of them can support a lie. But the complicated situation John described would be very difficult for two people to describe independently without there being a basis in fact. Even two smarties like John and Illanna."

"You said as far as it goes."

"Yes. Even if I am willing to accept the witch ritual at the cabin, it does not necessarily follow that they are involved in a devil cult here at the hospital."

"But I thought you said that Randy . . ."

"Randy's testimony isn't worth a damn."

Judy stamped her foot. "I know Randy. First of all, he is too simple to be devious. He wouldn't know how to lie. And second, I don't think he is smart enough to make up a story like that."

"John could."

Judy's eyes flashed angrily. "And you believe *that*?"

Schneider smiled. "No, I don't. That's the trouble. Personally, I don't believe John is at the bottom of any of this, but to prove it I need more evidence than stories of people accused of the crime and the testimony of an inmate."

"How are you going to get it?"

"I can't do much more here until I can get to see Illanna, and apparently I have to get a warrant to do that. I have to go back downtown and see the judge. I'll see you tonight."

III

John was back in his cell when Schneider
returned to the station house. It was late
afternoon. Schneider was a frustrated man.
The judge had been sympathetic but did not
feel that the warrant could be issued before
the hearing if the hospital did not want anyone
to talk to Illanna before that. Schneider was
apprehensive about telling John about
Illanna's situation, particularly since John's
predictions seemed to be more accurate than
his own.

John was moving restlessly around his cell
when Schneider entered. He came eagerly
over to the barred door when he saw the
lieutenant coming down the corridor. "How is
she?"

"She's fine."

"You talked to her?"

"Uh . . . not exactly."

"Why not?"

"She's undergoing tests . . . assessments they
call it . . . they don't want her disturbed before
the hearing."

"Bullshit. They can't keep anyone from talking to her." John paused ominously. "Where is she, Schneider?"

"Johnson thought it best that she go directly to the Long Term Care Center."

John turned white. He wasn't angry anymore. He was scared, scared to death for Illanna. Finally he spoke. "Don't you see what they are doing? They won't let you see her because they've got her so zonked on drugs you'd pull her out of there yourself if you saw her."

"John, don't be irrational. They can't harm her . . . not in there. Everything that happens to a patient is charted and documented. They are watched twenty four hours a day. She has to be safe."

"You poor fool! You think they play by your rules? They've got her and they can do anything they want with her, and you will never know what happened."

"John, I'm doing everything I can. I'm getting a warrant for access to her, and it will be coming through any time now . . . " Schneider trailed off lamely.

John looked at him hard. "You're beginning to get scared too, aren't you?"

"No . . . of course not," Schneider said defensively.

"Don't bullshit me, Bob."

"I'm not."

"Okay. I'll have to solve this problem myself."

"John, there is nothing you can do. I'll stay on top of it and keep prowling around up there until Illanna's hearing. They wouldn't dare pull anything with us watching them so closely."

"Sure." John turned away and stared out between the bars at the darkening sky.

"I'll see you tomorrow."

John didn't answer and Schneider walked dejectedly out of the cell block to make his report. Even the anticipation of an evening with Judy didn't cheer him up. He only had three friends in the world, and two of them were in deep trouble.

John ate his dinner and stared at the cell wall. He had already decided what to do, but he had to wait until lights out.

After supper the time dragged by interminably. At nine o'clock the lights went out. Shortly there were snores coming from the only other occupied cell. Quietly he pulled the bed away from the wall at one end and turned it perpendicular to the window.

John had little to do in the time since his return from the infirmary. He had spent much of that time inspecting his new surroundings. The jail looked like a very sturdy structure. It appeared to be made of solid brick, three courses interlocking from the outside to the inside. The bricks on the inside had been painted in the not too distant past, but some of the mortar had chipped away at the barred window and John noticed the mortar underneath had deteriorated in the two hundred-year old structure to the point where it was largely sand. It was then that he began toying with the idea of escape. It was only a fantasy at first, something to occupy his mind. The fantasy took on a real dimension when he heard about Illanna's predicament. His own situation seemed trivial to him compared to the dangers he imagined for her at the hospital.

Having the bed positioned tight against the cell door, he pulled the mattress over the end of the upper bunk. A space of approximately three feet remained between the end of the bed and the wall. John leaned back against the mattress and wedged his feet against the lintel just below the window. He took three deep breaths and began to push easily and then with greater and greater intensity. At first nothing happened. Beads of sweat popped out on John's brow. His face flushed, turned dark red and then began to take on a purplish hue as he held the last breath and increased the pressure. Still there was no give to the wall. He exhaled and brought his feet back to the floor. Everything seemed as it was. There were no cracks in the wall, nothing to indicate the almost 2000 pounds of pressure John was able to exert in that position. John studied the structure of the window more closely. The lintel at the bottom of the window interlocked with columns at the side of the window, probably steel reinforced, which in turn locked into the surrounding wall. Since the lintel was solid, the pressure would be distributed along the length and transmitted to the side of the window as well. He decided to try again with his feet below the lintel. He positioned himself slightly lower on the bed and placed his feet against the brick. This time, before he even reached maximum exertion, he felt the bricks giving beneath his feet. He eased off again.

Outside, the Municipal Parking Lot was quiet. John moved back and forth, getting as wide an angle as possible in surveying the situation outside. If the wall gave way it was bound to make some noise. There didn't seem to be anyone in or near the parking lot to stop him if he did get out, however.

Climbing the wall for the third time, he took three breaths again but instead of the gradual pressure he had been exerting, he exploded against the wall. The bricks beneath the window caved outward and fell into the parking lot beyond. The wall gave way so suddenly John almost fell to the floor. He grabbed the end of the bed as he slid and lowered himself down. Only a few bricks had fallen, and they had not made much noise. John listened anxiously for any activity in the building. Everything was quiet.

It was a simple matter, once the wall had been breached, to pull bricks out of the wall course after course. John worked quickly, throwing the bricks onto the lower bunk where they made no sound. Within two minutes the hole beneath the window was big enough for John to squeeze through. He hit the ground running. A single street light caught the running figure briefly, and John was gone into the darkness.

John rested in the shadows when he was several blocks from the jail house. His instinct was to go directly to the hospital, but without keys and in prison garb, his chances of helping Illanna were almost nil. He decided to chance going home. If his escape was not noticed for an hour, he could be in and out. He started running, pacing himself for the three miles to his suburban home.

When he reached the street, everything was quiet. No police cars, not even any cars he didn't recognize as belonging to his neighbors. He kept to the side of the street away from the street lights and hurried up the dark lane. The key was in its usual place, and he quickly ducked inside.

He didn't want to risk a light, so he fumbled around in the dining room until he located a flashlight in the cupboard and took it upstairs to change. As he pulled on a pair of Levis and a black turtleneck, he had a "deja vu" experience. He had done all this before.

It was unlikely that he could get the Jaguar out unnoticed, but the neighbors might not think anything of it, or if they did, they wouldn't know who to call or if they should call anyone. It was immaterial anyway. John needed the car to get to the hospital and to get Illanna away if he could.

The Jaguar turned over immediately and John was on his way to the hospital. Still no signs of police or sirens from the direction of the municipal complex. He pulled into the same spot he had two years before, only this time he headed for the Long Term Care Building instead of the Admission Ward.

He couldn't sneak into this Center. He didn't know exactly where Illanna was. John decided to try to bluff his way in. The lobby was dimly lit. The third shift charge nurse had her back to the door and looked up, startled, when John cleared his throat. She was not used to seeing anyone but Security at this time of night. She had on the tip of her tongue "Who the hell . . " but managed to come out with, "May I help you?"

John had never seen the woman before, which was probably a plus in the situation. "I'm . . . er . . . Dr. Lowell. I must see one of my clients."

The nurse raised her eyebrows but did not seem to recognize the name. That was a point in John's favor. She didn't know about his arrest. John was never more glad for the insular life most people on third shift led.

"I'm sorry . . . What is your business here?"

"I'm a psychologist here at the hospital. I was supposed to check on one of my clients today, and I missed the appointment."

The nurse was looking more skeptical by the minute. "This is highly irregular. Could I please see your credentials?"

John got out his wallet and showed her his State Employment Card and his Psychology License Card along with his Hospital Photo I.D.

She looked at the picture and hard at John. She seemed satisfied with the identification, but still puzzled by the request.

"Who did you want to see?"

"Illanna Romanowsky."

The eyebrows went up again. There was a note in the red book that Ms. Romanowsky was not allowed visitors. Of course, the psychologist was not a visitor, but . . . "Ms. Romanowsky is not allowed visitors, and I am sure at this hour she is asleep."

"It's very important that I see her tonight . . . just for a few minutes."

"I'm sorry, I'm going to have to check with the shift supervisor about this."

John considered vaulting over the counter and grabbing the record, but then the nurse pulled a card out of a file box and turned her back on John while she dialed the Supervisor. In the upper right hand corner John saw the room number -- 215. That's all he needed. He ran over to the elevator and turned his key in the lock. The elevator was on the first floor and the doors opened immediately.

The sound spun the nurse around. "Wait a minute. Where do you think you're . . ."

The doors closed and John was on his way to the second floor. The elevator door opened and John threw the emergency lock switch to "hold." As he stepped out into the hall the door at the far end of the hall was just closing. He ran down the hall, hastily checking the room numbers. He reached 215 and opened the door. The room was empty. He tried to get a grip on himself. Security would be here in minutes. They would know about him. They might already be in touch with the police. Where was she?

Then he remembered the closing door. He rushed to the fire tower exit and down the stairs. He was about to open the first floor door when he heard a noise below him. The basement. Down another flight of stairs. He hesitated outside of the door of the basement, listening. He opened the door as quietly as he could. There was no mistaking the hulking figure at the far end of the room. Randy. Draped over his shoulder, black hair streaming almost to the floor, was Illanna. A cry caught in his throat as the linen shelves swung back behind them. They were gone. John tore the length of the basement and clawed at the shelves but could not find the release mechanisms. Seconds were ticking away. Randy could be lost in the labyrinth of tunnels within a few of those precious seconds. John gnashed his teeth in frustration. Then he began to think. He had not been aware of a tunnel from this room, but it must connect with the main tunnel which ran at ninety degrees to the Long Term Care Center and Geriatrics. John raced up the steps to the fire exit.

The alarm bell began to sound as soon as the outside door opened. John was past caring. He sprinted up the hill to the Geriatrics Building, burst through the front door and past an amazed charge nurse. In seconds he was down in the basement, running toward the Psychiatric Treatment Center. John had been down this tunnel many times in bad weather. It was the same -- summer and winter, day and night -- the dim overhead lights vanishing into the receding gloom. There was a difference this time, however. The tunnel seemed to come to a stop in the middle. Too late John saw what it was. Some sort of door had opened and was blocking off the tunnel. While he was still 50 yards away, the door swung shut. When he reached the spot where he thought the door should be, there was nothing but a blank, brick wall. He examined the wall carefully. The bricks were arranged in panels with vertical metal strips every four feet. One of the panels must be a door, but which one?

John looked around desperately. Above him were the steam pipes which went to all the buildings from the main power plant. Wedged between two of them was a four foot section of one inch pipe. John pulled it down and tapped the three panels which were in the general area where he had seen the door close. The middle one sounded different . . . hollow.

Using the pipe like a digging iron, John attacked the wall. It was slow going. The minutes were slipping by, and he still hadn't breached the wall. He wasn't even positive that there was a passage behind the panel. He began to panic. If there were other passages beyond this, he wouldn't know which one to take. The eerie image of Illanna draped over Randy's shoulder kept flashing through his mind. Medieval like the Hunchback of Notre Dame. Randy's cruel nickname was coming true with a vengeance. Where was he taking her and why? Someone must be leading him and operating the doors. Rachel? Fortunado?

John kept pounding away at the bricks. Now they began to crumble under the onslaught. The ones in the middle of the panel were breaking loose. They fell away into a hollow space. Soon John could look through, and in the blackness, far away, he could see a pin point of light. He redoubled his efforts. Bricks were coming out two or three at a blow now. In a few minutes the hole was big enough for John to squeeze through. He started running toward the light. He hit the walls of the passage and almost fell several times before his eyes adjusted to the inky blackness of the tunnel. The light was bigger now but still dim and flickering.

John crashed into an iron gate at the end of the tunnel. He was knocked back, stunned for an instant. The picture he saw when he staggered back to the gate was a scene from hell. A black hooded figure stood with its back to the metal gate. A white hand held a knife high in the air, glinting in the flickering candle light. A naked body lay on a stone altar. Just as John hit the gate, Illanna screamed. John grabbed at the bars, trying to rip them out of the wall. "Illanna!"

Rachel turned toward the sound. Her black eyes were glassy, feverish with lust and hate. She stared, unseeing, at the desperate psychologist and turned back to the altar. The sing-song cadence began again. In the background, a devil's figure was hopping from one foot to the other in frustration and indecision. If he called out to Rachel, John would recognize his voice. If he didn't stop her, he was an accessory to a witnessed murder. Rachel paid no attention to him or John. She was into the ritual with a singleness of purpose which excluded everything outside the pentagram.

John kept tugging at the gate, but the steel bars held. Then he remembered Randy. Randy was huddled off to the side of the room, swaying back and forth, crying and mumbling to himself.

"Randy!"

The hulking figure turned toward the sound. He stared at John, a puzzled look coming over his face. He was fighting the drugged fog, trying to remember.

"Randy! It's Illanna! Help her!"

Recognition spread across the stupefied face.
The massive hulk turned toward the black-
robed figure. Suddenly the room seemed to
tremble. The stone altar began to slide away
from Rachel. Beneath it yawned an opening
pit. A sulfurous smoke spewed forth into the
chamber. Rachel screamed and turned
toward Randy, knife still high in the air.
Randy grunted a guttural sound and swept
her aside as if she were a paper doll. She
slipped and fell into the opening. Her scream
went on and on, fading into the depths of the
earth. The smoke filled the chamber.

John could no longer see anything in the
room. He was choking on the smoke when
hands seized him from behind. All at once he
was surrounded by security guards and
Schneider was by his side.

"What's happening?"

"Illanna's in there . . . Rachel . . ."

"Get the gate open!"

One of the Security guards shone his
flashlight on the lock.

"Maybe one of the old skeleton keys will work
on it." He tried two. The third one turned in

the lock, and the gate swung open. The smoke was beginning to settle. Randy was huddled next to the altar. Illanna was still strapped on top. Schneider quickly threw a coat over her while John worked at the straps. A red, robed figure lay sprawled beside the devil's sarcophagus on the far side of the chamber. One of the security guards leaned over him.

"Hey! This guy is dead!"

Schneider bent over the robed figure and removed the devil's mask. It was Fortunado, his head twisted at a grotesque angle.

"His neck is broken. John, I thought you said Rachel . . ."

"She was here. She fell into some kind of a pit beneath the altar."

Schneider inspected the altar. He tried to push it aside, but it wouldn't budge. "This thing must weigh a ton. How could it have moved?"

"I don't know. I yelled for Randy to stop Rachel."

"Stop her from what?"

"She had a knife and was about to . . ."

Schneider shuddered. Illanna was sobbing into John's shoulder.

Schneider took charge. "Let's get her and Randy out of here. Two of you stay with the body and I'll send my men along."

CHAPTER TEN -- MALLEUS

I

The third shift charge nurse for the Geriatrics Unit made up the bed in the sick room for Illanna. Two of the aides escorted Randy back to his ward. Schneider and John went back to John's office. Schneider made a couple of calls to get his crew to the Hospital.

"I suppose I have to go back to jail?" John was beginning to relax now that Illanna and Randy were safe.

"Not necessarily. They're not too happy with your reconstruction of the Court House. On the other hand, they won't want a hassle with false arrest. You have pretty well vindicated yourself as far as the Malleus business goes."

"What about breaking out of jail?"

"Like I said, they are not too happy about it. But they are going to be stuck with the fact that if you hadn't escaped Illanna would be dead, and they sent her back here. Since you hadn't been arraigned yet, I think I can get the Chief to drop the whole thing. When you're up to it, I'd like you to tell me exactly what went on tonight."

"I'm okay now that Illanna's out of danger, but I'm worried about Randy."

"Randy will never be charged with murder under these circumstances."

"No, it's not that . . . It's everything he's been through in the last few days. I'm not sure how it's going to affect him."

"John, I'm sorry . . ."

"Don't be. You did what you had to do. The difference between us was that you only had suspicions about Fortunado and Rachel. I *knew* they were up to something because of what Illanna and I saw up at the cabin."

"I could have believed you."

"Sure. But what about your Chief?"

"You've got a point."

"When you told me Illanna had been admitted to the Long Term Care Unit, I knew Fortunado and Rachel had engineered it. It is a marked departure from hospital policy. Your inability to get to see her not only confirmed that suspicion but made it probable that she was in no condition to see *you*. I had to get her out."

"Again?"

John chuckled wryly. "Yes. I was the one who helped her escape two years ago."

"Why?"

"She didn't belong here."

"Do you sneak in at night and smuggle every patient out who doesn't belong?"

"No."

"Then why her?"

"Two reasons. Not only didn't she belong, but her experience here could have damaged her emotionally. More importantly, though, a member of the staff tried to rape her and might have succeeded if he got another chance."

"Surely the hospital can protect patients from that kind of abuse!"

"You would think so, but the circumstances were unusual and Johnson was preoccupied with other matters at the time."

"Let's get back to tonight.

"The building is old. Braced against a bed in a half squat position I can exert around a ton of pressure on a few square inches of surface."

"There is also some embarrassment about that downtown. I imagine your demonstration is going to end up costing the City a lot of money."

John laughed. "Anyway, after I got out I didn't have much of a plan except to get Illanna out of here. I went home and changed and got the car. I got up in the ward just in time to see Randy taking Illanna down to the basement of the Long Term Care Building."

"Then?"

"At first all I saw was Randy carrying Illanna. I knew he must be with someone else, because someone had to be opening the doors. I figured it must be Rachel, because she is the only other person beside myself who has any influence over him."

"Where did they get into the tunnel system?"

"Through a tunnel which isn't used anymore connecting with the main tunnel between the Geriatrics Unit and the Administration building."

"You followed them?"

"I couldn't. They have some arrangement with the laundry shelves which blocks the door. I didn't have time to figure it out, so I tried to intercept them in the main tunnel."

"And?"

"I was too late again, but I saw where the tunnel opened up."

"We saw the job you did on that . . . you're into demolition tonight."

"It took quite a bit of time though . . . almost too much." John shuddered, remembering the knife.

"Who was in the chamber when you got there?"

"At first I saw only Illanna on the altar and a black-robed figure. I wasn't paying much attention to anything else. I called out, and Rachel turned around. She was . . . I don't know . . . in some kind of trance . . . I guess associated with the ritual. It didn't look like my being there affected her one way or the other. I saw Randy, yelled to him to help Illanna, and he went toward Rachel and the altar."

"Then what happened?"

"It's very confusing. . . it all happened so fast. Just as Randy started toward Rachel, the altar swung back away from Rachel. Randy brushed against her, and she fell into a hole underneath. A yellow smoke came out of the pit, and I couldn't see anything else."

"That's when we arrived?"

"Yes."

"What about Fortunado?"

"I saw him in the background but wasn't paying any attention to him."

"Why do you suppose Randy attacked him?"

"Did he?"

"He must have. He was the only person in the room beside Illanna, and she was strapped to the altar."

John was silent. He looked troubled.

Schneider continued. "We can ask Illanna when she wakes up."

"I don't think she is going to be able to tell you much. She seemed to be pretty heavily sedated. Remember, I had to carry her back here, and then she was out like a light in spite of what she had just been through."

"But she was awake during . . ."

"Only for a moment."

"We can question Randy."

"Yes . . . but they had him zonked too or they never could have gotten him to take Illanna down there. I doubt if he even knew it was her or what he was doing."

"Why do you suppose they involved him?"

"They probably would have cooked something up about the two of them escaping."

"Well, it's not very tidy, and we are going to have to tie them into the other two murders, but they are much better candidates than you and Illanna at this point."

"Thanks!"

"You know I haven't thought you were guilty for some time. Why don't you get some rest? I'll see what I can do downtown about getting you officially released . . . and Illanna too."

John nodded and stumbled to the couch in the corner of his office.

II

When John woke, the sun was streaming through his window. His first thought was of Illanna. He went out into the hall and over to the nursing station. Judy was smiling broadly.

"Good morning, Doctor."

"Hi, Judy . . . How's . . .?"

"She's still asleep. The injection should be wearing off, though. Why don't you go on in?"

John didn't need any encouragement. He entered the small bedroom at the rear of the nursing station which was used as a sick room for the Geriatrics Ward. It was also set up as an isolation room so there were no windows. A complicated air circulation system kept a negative air flow through a filter system to the outside. A small light on the stand next to the bed illuminated the sleeping figure. The pale face provided no hint of the harrowing experiences of the night before. John sat in the chair next to the bed for a long time watching her and finally nodded off to sleep again himself. When he woke it was with a start from sleeping in the unusual position. Illanna was looking at him and smiling.

"Morning, love."

John was on his knees next to the bed hugging her in an instant. "Are you all right?"

"Sort of groggy. They gave me a shot."

"I know. Do you remember anything about last night?"

"I had a dream. Rachel was bending over me with a knife. I screamed, and you were there and Randy and the devil. It's all mixed up."

"It wasn't a dream."

"No, I guess it wasn't, but it seemed like one."

"It's because of the medication. You were pretty far under."

"What happened?"

John related the events as he knew them and asked, "Do you know what happened after Rachel fell?"

"No, I didn't even know she did. She just sort of disappeared, and then there was that choking smoke."

"And you didn't see anything else?"

Illanna forced herself to think back. "I couldn't see anything, but I did hear a scuffle behind the altar."

"Near the sarcophagus?"

"I guess so."

"That must have been Fortunado struggling with Randy."

"Randy? Did he kill Fortunado?"

"He must have. There was no one else in the room."

Illanna looked at John a long time before she replied. "Don't be too sure of that, John."

"What do you mean?"

"That there wasn't some . . . something else in the room."

"Some*thing*?"

"What do you think Rachel was trying to do in the room?"

"Kill you."

"That's true, but she wasn't just trying to kill me."

"What then?"

"She was trying to sacrifice me."

"I don't see the difference."

"The difference is in the purpose. She wanted to get rid of me, but she was doing it in the context of devil worship."

"So?"

"John, from the nature of that room and what Randy described, they have been trying to conjure up the devil."

"Okay, but I don't see how that relates to Fortunado's death."

"Where was he standing?"

"I told you. Back by the sarcophagus."

"Outside the pentagram?"

John thought a moment. "The body was, yes, when we checked it."

"Then it's possible she succeeded."

"Succeeded in what?"

"Conjuring up the devil."

"Oh, come on!"

"You still don't believe, do you?"

"I believe in you. I believe in your psychic powers. I'm beginning to believe that everyone has them to a degree, including myself. But I can't believe in devils."

Illanna sighed. "I guess it is too much to expect. Even if it's true, it wouldn't help Randy, because no one else would believe it."

"Randy doesn't need help in that regard anyway."

"No?"

"The circumstances certainly exonerate him. Both Rachel and Fortunado were clearly trying to kill you. Also, Randy was so heavily drugged he was not responsible for anything he did. He will never be brought to trial for either Rachel's or Fortunado's death."

"Well that's something, anyway."

"I'm still worried about him."

"The experience?"

"Yes. He was doing so well before all of this happened. I don't know how it's going to affect him."

"I'm sure you can straighten him out again."

"I hope so. I'd like to see him out of here."

"Could he make it on the outside?"

"With help."

"Yours?"

"Yes."

"John, can you do that? With your responsibilities in here, can you afford to work with him on the outside?"

"I think my responsibilities in here are about over."

"You're cleared of the murders aren't you?"

"Oh, yes. Bob's downtown now getting it all straightened out." John paused and looked away.

Illanna's face fell. "Oh . . . You mean me."

"I'm afraid the system will not forgive me for getting you out of here before."

"But, John, you can explain all that."

"I know. But it's just not the way things are done."

"I'm sorry John. I've . . ."

"Don't be. In the first place, if I hadn't, we never would have gotten together, and that means more to me than any job, or even my career. In the second place, I was beginning to get bored with the job even before this. Afterwards, I don't think I could go back to the day-to-day routine."

"So what are you going to do?"

"What are *we* going to do? You're not getting away from me again . . . ever." John looked at her in the way he had only ever been able to look at her when she was asleep.

"I love you too, John. Do you think we will ever see eye to eye on . . ."

"I doubt it, but it doesn't matter. I was miserable all the time you were gone. No philosophical difference can change that. I am never going to try and change you again."

"And you don't mind if I believe..."

"No. I don't even mind if you try to get *me* to believe in devils or angels or any creatures under or over the earth. Just don't leave me again."

"I won't John . . . ever."

"Speaking of which, I still can't buy Rachel actually conjuring up the devil, but it has given me another idea I'd like to check out."

"What's that?"

"Well . . . Sherlock Holmes used to say 'if you rule out every other possibility, then the one that's left must be true.'"

"Meaning?"

"Suppose we assume that Randy didn't kill Fortunado."

"Okay."

"Then someone else . . ."

"Or something else . . ."

"Then something or someone else must have been in the room."

"So?"

"So how did it get in and out?"

"The pit."

"Maybe. But there might be another entrance to that chamber we don't know about. I'm going to go back down there and check it out."

"Be careful John."

"I will. Judy will look after you. I'll tell her where I'm going so Bob can catch up with me if he's interested." John kissed her and went

out to the nursing station to relay his plan to
Judy.

III

The trip back to the chamber was considerably different from the one the night before. John was unhurried and relaxed as he traversed the main tunnel to the point where he had breached the wall. Temporary electric lines had been run from the main tunnel to the chamber, and several detectives were going over the area with a fine-tooth comb. When John arrived, the altar was again slid back, exposing the rectangular hole in the floor. John introduced himself and almost laughed at the look of awe on their faces. It wasn't much more than twelve hours since he had broken out of jail, and he was already a legend. "Have you found Rachel yet?"

"No."

"No?"

"I don't think we ever will."

"Why not?"

The big detective doing the talking pointed to a string tied to the corner of the altar and hanging down into the pit. "That string is 500 feet long and it doesn't reach the bottom of the hole."

"You're kidding!"

"Nope. If she's down there, she's going to stay."

"Couldn't there be a side passage off the main shaft?"

"I don't know about farther down, but you can see for fifty to seventy-five feet with the light, and it's solid rock."

"Can't you lower a light and a remote TV camera?"

"Sure, and we might. But it's going to get expensive, and five hundred feet is a long way down. We're going to have problems getting all the equipment down into this small room. I don't think we're ever going to see the bottom of that hole, never mind recover a body from it."

"So?"

"So, like I said, if she's down there, it's likely there she stays."

John took another look at the altar. "How does this thing work?"

"That's another thing. It doesn't."

"It doesn't what?"

"It doesn't work. There's no sliding mechanism, no bearing. Nothing. Just a couple of tons of rock sitting on that hole."

"How did you move it?"

"With that." The detective pointed to a hand winch attached to a bolt ring on the side of the altar.

"How did it move last night?"

"Are you sure it did?"

"I saw it swing back."

"Well, it took a hell of a shove to do it."

John laughed.

"What's the joke?"

"I was just thinking of someone who agrees with you."

"I don't get it."

"Neither do I. Do you mind if I look around for a while?"

"Help yourself. The technicians are through, and there's nothing much to disturb anyway."

The only part of the wall which was different from the rest was the sarcophagus which protruded from the smooth stones. John started with a close inspection of the bronze image. Looking through the red glass eye, he could see that the interior was hollow but not much else. He called the detective over. "Did anyone try to open this up?"

"Open it?"

"Yes. Sarcophagi are usually hollow to hold a body. This one seems to be also."

"Let me see." The detective looked through the eye and then shone his flashlight around. "It's hollow all right, but I don't see any way to open it."

John felt over the surface of the statue. When he got to the trident, he pulled on it and it came toward him. There was a click, and the left side of the sarcophagus came away from the wall.

"Well I'll be damned!"

"We probably all will," replied John and swung the cover all the way open. The inside was smooth. When John pushed on the back, it swung away easily, revealing the room beyond. So there *was* another way in! "I wonder where this leads?"

"We'd better wait for Schneider. He didn't say anything about exploring any more tunnels."

"He knows I'm down here. I'd like to follow this and see where it goes."

"I don't know . . ."

John persisted.

"Well, I can't stop you. It's your hospital, but don't get lost."

John spent only a moment in the small room behind the idol. He lifted the latch in the door at the back of the room and began the long ascent in the tunnel beyond. He tried to orient himself with respect to the hospital grounds but gave it up. The tunnels were all at odd angles to each other, and with the two circular rooms he had gone through, it was hard to figure the relationship to the main tunnel. At last he came to a metal door, went through the isolation cell, and stood in the hydrotherapy room. He still didn't know where he was. He recognized the nature of the room, which was replicated in the basement of all of the older buildings, but didn't recognize this particular one. Then he looked out of the basement window and saw the Admission Building across the street. This was the

Administration Building! So that's how
Fortunado got around. It was certainly
helpful to Schneider's case, but it didn't solve
Fortunado's murder, or did it?

And Moses said, "Let my people go." A myriad
of images flickered through John's mind, and
everything fell into place.

IV

"Hello, John," 'God' sat on his throne, his long white hair hanging over his leisure coat. "I'm glad to see you. Schneider called and said everything was straightened out."

"He thinks it is."

A shadow passed over the placid face. "And you don't?"

"No."

"Why?"

"It doesn't make sense. Why would Fortunado and Rachel want to kill Azahdi and Goldstein? What's the connection between them? Why would they want to have something on me? None of it hangs together."

"Well, it's pretty obvious that Fortunado and Rachel were running some kind of sex/devil cult. Maybe Azahdi found out about it."

"Okay. But how was Goldstein involved?"

"Does he have to be? Rachel and Dick were into sex games, witchcraft, devil worship, and human sacrifice. Does it all have to be rational?"

"No. Not if there isn't some other rational explanation."

"Why don't you leave well enough alone, John? You are cleared. Illanna will be out of here, and maybe I can get Central Office to overlook your . . . er . . . indiscretion two years ago."

"I can't leave it alone. Randy will be held responsible for Fortunado's death and maybe Rachel's as well."

"He will never be brought to trial."

"That's true enough, but he will have it hanging over his head all of his life, and it may keep him from ever getting out of here."

"Should he be out of here?"

"Yes . . . I think so."

Johnson's face retained its composed look, but hatred flickered behind his eyes. "You are all so preoccupied with getting patients out of here, aren't you? Out of here to what? The community doesn't want them. They wander the streets without food or shelter until they become a nuisance, then they get sent back here, to jail, or maybe die."

"That's it, isn't it?"

"What?"

"The connection between Azahdi and Goldstein. They were both pushing to get all of the patients out of here and close the place down. Deinstitutionalization."

The hidden anger exploded to the surface. "Deinstitutionalization. Ha! The ultimate hypocrisy. Society refuses to tolerate deviant behavior, so they put the transgressors away. The institution has to tolerate the behavior, so the environment is arranged to withstand it and change it. The patient 'adjusts' to the protected environment and is 'institutionalized'. But treatment is expensive. When patients were warehoused at $5.00 a day on stinking wards, chained to their beds for lack of staff to control them, no one in the community protested. But now we're 'regulated'. We have doctors and nurses and psychologists and social workers and activity aides and a therapeutic environment. At what cost? Two hundred dollars a day, seventy thousand dollars a year per patient. Now institutionalization is bad. It demeans. It deprives of liberty and rights. Put them back on the streets! Do you know what Azahdi and Goldstein were up to?"

"No," said John softly.

"They were buying up the boarding homes through third parties. Goldstein masterminded the whole thing. He probably had his Azahdis in every hospital in the state. While he was busy downtown keeping the boarding homes from being regulated and inspected, the Azahdis were pushing the patients out to fill them up, with Social Security, Medicare and Medical Assistance paying five times what the service was worth. Goldstein must have cleared a million dollars a year. That's why they had to get something on you."

"I don't get it."

"You were getting too close. You were asking questions about the placements, the conditions of the homes. They had to get some leverage on you to back off. Azahdi found out about Illanna."

"You're Malleus, aren't you?"

"Yes, dammit, I'm Malleus. The hammer *for* witches not *of* them. In medieval days, they called the schizophrenics witches and drove them out into the wastelands to die of exposure. They had no one to protect them.

They do now." Johnson slumped back into his chair.

"You could have blown the whistle on Goldstein."

"And who would care? They all want them out. Warehoused again in hovels this time instead of State Hospitals. I'm sorry you had to find out, John. I'm afraid I am not going to be able to let you out of here with that knowledge."

Johnson rose from his chair, and with the agility bred from years of karate training, leapt between John and the door. John backed away toward the far wall. He tried to get Johnson talking again.

"Why did you kill Fortunado?"

"I didn't."

Johnson took two steps and leapt for John's head, feet first. John tried to duck off to the right.

"Johnson!" Schneider was in the doorway. Johnson's head snapped toward the sound, turning his body away from its target. His feet collided with John's shoulder and grazed off to the left into the window behind him. The glass and casing exploded outward. He never made a sound. John turned in time to see him hit the fountain three floors below. By the time Schneider got across the room, he lay motionless . . . broken on the stone center. John had never noticed before that the fountain was in the shape of a pentagram.

V

The four of them sat in Schneider's apartment. It was the first time he had ever had "friends over." He was enjoying the normalcy of it. Judy kept jumping up and running into the kitchen for drinks or dip, and Schneider beamed at her and John and Illanna. John could hardly keep from laughing at the contrast of this man and the uptight neurotic he had met only a few days before. He probably could have laughed, and Schneider would have known he was laughing for him and not at him. They were sorting out the events at the hospital which had come to such a dramatic climax on Friday.

"What's going to happen to Randy?" Schneider asked.

"I'm going to get him released from the hospital as soon as possible."

"He didn't suffer any ill effects from the medication and . . .?" Schneider could hardly bring himself to talk about the grisly scene in the devil chamber.

"No. He was so zonked by the drugs that, like Illanna, the events do not have a real quality for him. He hardly remembers what happened."

"The District Attorney didn't press charges, like we figured."

"I still don't like either Rachel's or Fortunado's deaths being attributed to him, though," said John.

"Does Randy have family?"

"No."

"Then who is going to take care of him on the outside?"

"We are," said Illanna. "Maybe it's the other way around. If he hadn't taken care of me, I wouldn't be here."

"That's a big responsibility."

"Any bigger than taking care of a mother?" John said, looking directly at Schneider.

"No."

"It's not just Randy saving Illanna's life. He's a friend of ours who needs some help, and we can give it to him."

"What about your standing with the State?"

"They have asked me to resign from State service."

"Are you going to?"

"I don't know. I could probably fight it, but I'm not sure I want to."

"No?"

"No. I had been getting stale on that job. I think it's time to start something new."

"Like what?"

"I haven't decided yet."

"Judy and I have been talking about what you two did in all this and have concluded that you were always at least one step ahead of me in seeing what was going on."

"Well, I had been up at the hospital for years."

"It's not just that. You seemed to know where to look and at whom."

"That was Illanna. She was on to Rachel before she ever met her, and she also proved Fortunado was involved in the devil cult."

"How?"

"You wouldn't believe me if I told you."

"You mean the E.S.P. stuff?"

"Yes."

"Don't be too sure. We use psychics all the time. Three times in the last year on missing person cases. It's done all over the country."

"Well, she knew someone was into witchcraft and devil worship at the hospital before she ever met Rachel, and she knew what was going on at Fortunado's cabin before she ever saw it."

"John's giving me too much credit. He's the one who figured everything out. Johnson had passed me completely."

"Not really. You felt his presence from the beginning but got confused once I zeroed in on Fortunado and Rachel."

"Well, don't argue," laughed Schneider. "You two make a pretty good team."

"Don't we," smiled Illanna, putting her arm through John's.

"There are still some things I don't understand," said Schneider.

"Like what?"

"About Johnson's motivation. Why didn't he simply let someone know what he suspected about Goldstein and Azahdi instead of killing them?"

"That's because you don't understand the nature of the true paranoid. Johnson was the perfect person in the perfect place to develop the delusion system that he had. He was highly intelligent and very introspective. The nature of his job isolated him from society. When he first became superintendent (forty years ago), State Hospitals were like feudal fiefdoms. The superintendent had absolute authority over what went on inside the gates. No one reviewed what was happening as long as the hospital didn't go over budget, and the budget was damned small. Johnson was a very compassionate man. He not only cared about his patients, but he cared about how they lived. Over the years he became very protective of them. They became 'his people'. That worked out well for him and for them. He improved the situation in the hospital and maintained his position of power. Starting in the sixties, though, things began to change. Because of the discovery of psychotropic medication, some patients were able to make it in the community even though there was really no 'cure' for their condition. As long as they stayed on their medication, their behavior was under control . . . a sort of pharmacological straight jacket. The population of State Hospitals began to decline, slowly at first, and then more rapidly. Deinstitutionalization they called it. On balance, deinstitutionalization was probably a good thing, but it produced a lot of human misery too. The plan was to shift the care from inpatient facilities to outpatient facilities with supportive living arrangements. It was going to be cheaper, and the patients were going to live more independent and productive lives."

"What went wrong?" Schneider asked.

"Several things. First, they overestimated the effectiveness of the drugs. Several states closed the State Hospitals altogether, but a hard core of patients, about twenty percent, could not make it on the outside under any circumstances. No long term facilities had been developed in the community to take care of them. Second, when the Mental Health Act under Kennedy's Administration funded the Community Mental Health Programs, it was only seed money. Once the programs had been developed, the states were supposed to take over the funding with the money they were saving by not having to run State Hospitals. But they discovered a whole new population in the community which snapped up the services, and the State Hospital patients were left out in the cold literally. Finally, the long term effects of psychotropics gave us a large number of chronically debilitated patients who had to be cared for."

"Where are the patients now?"

"Twenty-five percent are in some sort of inpatient facilities. Twenty-five percent are in jail (for every hospital bed we've closed down, we have opened at least two beds in jails), and the rest are on the street or in flophouses somewhere. Anyway, Johnson had to deal with these attacks on his kingdom. More and more, society became the enemy. He became more and more protective of 'his people'. When he got into Goldstein's and Azahdi's scheme, he finally had a focus for his paranoia. Malleus the Avenger of Witches was born."

"I guess I can understand all that, but there is still one part of the puzzle which doesn't fit."

"You mean Fortunado's and Rachel's deaths," said John.

"Yes. Randy could have done it, but he doesn't remember. Johnson had access to the room and admitted to the other murders but denied involvement in Fortunado's and Rachel's deaths. Under the circumstances, there is no reason why he should have lied. Randy must have done it."

"Not necessarily," said John, looking at Illanna.